"T... reading and writing. The books changed my life."
—*Gavin T.*

"Bluford books are stories that kids and teens can relate to. Readers can use them to build courage and find solutions to their problems—instead of giving up. They are a true inspiration."
—*Michelle M.*

"I am a HUGE fan of the Bluford Series. These books are so real and have impacted me in sooooo many positive ways."
—*Aaliyah H.*

"The Bluford Series is seriously amazing. These books made me want to read more and get off my phone."
—*Ricky M.*

"I love that these books are about the hardships young people face. They show we are resilient and can overcome anything."
—*Kennedy T.*

"I love these books. When you read them, you'll think you're inside a movie."
—*Pluto R.*

"I found it very easy to lose myself in these books. They kept my interest from beginning to end and were always realistic. The characters are vivid, and the endings left me in eager anticipation of the next book."
—*Keziah J.*

"These are life-changing stories that make you think long after you reach the last page."
—*Eddie M.*

"I'm loving the Bluford Series! I have never been so interested in books until now. These stories are amazing!"
—*Katherine B.*

"The Bluford books comforted me growing up. They brought me a sense of belonging and understanding when I most needed it."
—*Osman M.*

"I am obsessed with the Bluford Series. I relate to all the stories, and I experienced some of the same situations growing up and at school. These books helped me get my life together."
—*Jean L.*

"Each Bluford book gives you a story that could happen to anyone. The details make you feel like you are inside the books. The storylines are amazing and realistic. I loved them all."
—*Elpiclio B.*

"These books are 🔥. They got me through middle school."
—*Aaron T.*

"I love how Bluford books take risks by addressing tough topics. They may be controversial, but they are relatable to kids going through the same things. That's one of the reasons I enjoy them. They're *real*."
—*Mia M.*

On the Run

Karyn Langhorne Folan

Series Editor: Paul Langan

TOWNSEND PRESS
www.townsendpress.com

Books in the Bluford Series

Lost and Found
A Matter of Trust
Secrets in the Shadows
Someone to Love Me
The Bully
The Gun
Until We Meet Again
Blood Is Thicker
Brothers in Arms
Summer of Secrets
The Fallen
Shattered

Search for Safety
No Way Out
Schooled
Breaking Point
The Test
Pretty Ugly
Promises to Keep
Survivor
Girls Like Me
The Chosen
Alone
On the Run

Copyright © 2025 by Townsend Press, Inc.
Printed in the United States of America

9 8 7 6 5 4 3 2 1

Cover illustration © 2025 by Gerald Purnell

All rights reserved. Any one chapter
of this book may be reproduced without
the written permission of the publisher.
For permission to reproduce more than
one chapter, send requests to:

Townsend Press, Inc.
439 Kelley Drive
West Berlin, NJ 08091
permissions@townsendpress.com

ISBN: 978-1-59194-814-8

Library of Congress Control Number:
2025900440

Chapter 1

"We're live right now! Y'all seeing how to live the Lux Life! For real!"

Naveah Kendricks sat hunched at her desk so that Ms. Sherman, her ninth-grade English teacher at Bluford High, wouldn't see the phone in her lap. Naveah's black braids hung over the side of her face, hiding the single earbud in her ear. She had turned the volume low—as quiet as she could manage and still hear snippets of music and bits of conversation. One of her favorite influencers, Klassy Kay, was live streaming. Naveah wished she could turn it up so she could hear every word.

Klassy looked amazing, as usual. Her makeup was perfectly contoured, her hair extensions curled in ringlets on her shoulders, and her glossy nails gleamed like black talons sparkled with glitter. Klassy wore a designer top with cutouts that showed her curves and glowing caramel skin. In the background, Naveah spotted servers in black ties rushing between fancy tables arranged with wine glasses and silverware.

"We're at one of the most famous restaurants in L.A.," Klassy cooed to the camera. Her voice was smooth and excited, but not too excited. Naveah had practiced Klassy's tone many times. True, she didn't have the designer wardrobe or the followers, but Klassy's style was something she felt she could almost imitate.

We live from Bluford High right now! she imagined herself saying. For a second, Naveah pictured what it would be like to have thousands of followers watching her. The idea made her pulse quicken. But what would she say?

There was no way she would show them her dull classroom or her small, cluttered house where Christian, her eight-year-old brother, played video games after school. *Too boring*, she figured. Then an idea hit her. Maybe she could copy Klassy's voice and style but post about Bluford's cafeteria instead. It would be a joke, of course, but it might be funny.

This here's one of the most famous eateries in the 'hood, she'd say, pointing out the teachers on lunch duty as if they were celebrities. *That's right, Mr. Mitchell gets his mushy fruit salad right here on Tuesdays*, she could say. *And Mr. Dooling loves square pizza on Fridays even though it's almost too greasy to pick up.* The post would be silly but maybe she could tag Klassy. If Klassy "liked" it, Naveah hoped maybe she could get more followers. Maybe then someone would finally notice her.

Naveah studied Klassy Kay's face carefully as Ms. Sherman continued her unit on fairy tales and what they could teach to modern society. Today's talk was about *The Ugly Duckling*. Naveah could not care less.

What kind of filter will give me Klassy's look? she wondered. She closed the live stream and quickly snapped a selfie from her lap. The camera angle made her face look strangely puffy. She took another, raising her eyebrows and sucking in her cheeks.

Better, she thought.

Naveah applied one filter after another to the photo, finally settling on a look that smoothed her skin and made her lips seem glossy and wet. She uploaded the pic to Snapchat and waited for reactions. Naveah didn't have many followers, but hopefully, her cousins would click "like" and so would old friends from elementary and middle school if they were online. Lately, though, they responded less and less to her posts.

"Desmond's right," Ms. Sherman declared, heading to the whiteboard. "This is a story about the dangers of trying to be something you're not—and never discovering who you really are." The teacher drew a circle, then a square, and then an equal sign on the whiteboard. Then she drew a slash through the equal sign and began walking the aisles between desks. "Anyone ever felt like that? Like they don't fit?"

A few students shrugged, but others made grunting noises. Naveah held back a yawn and covered her phone as the teacher passed by.

"I know I have," Ms. Sherman admitted. She was small and wiry. From afar, Naveah thought she looked more like a student than a teacher. "People are not all the same, and we don't need to be! But still we are always trying to squeeze into boxes that others set up for us. It's like a girl on the soccer team who can run fast but can't dribble. Soccer doesn't fit for her. Why? Because she belongs on the track team, that's why!" she joked. "Track is where she fits!"

A few students smiled, while others rolled their eyes. Ms. Sherman coached girls track and cross country at Bluford High. She was always bringing up running in class and trying to recruit girls for her teams. Girls track had come close to winning All City championships this year, partly because of two girls in Naveah's class: Malika Shaw and Jonique Howard. Malika was always low-key about winning the 100-meter sprint. But Jonique? She bragged about her victories in the 800-meter and mile races constantly, even in class. Ms. Sherman never stopped her.

Naveah could still remember when the video blew up on Instagram a few weeks ago. Jonique standing sweaty and triumphant in her Bluford track uniform, holding her gold medal out at the camera as if she was an Olympic champion.

"Winning, baby!" she had hollered and then whooped joyfully, her hair braided into neat cornrows.

Like running fast is hard, Naveah thought at the time with a mixture of jealousy and annoyance that still lingered. Back in seventh grade, Naveah had beaten Jonique in a race around the field in gym class. That was years ago, but Naveah savored the memory whenever Jonique gloated, which seemed to be almost every day.

Naveah glanced over at the two runners. Malika sat on the far side of class, still smiling from Ms. Sherman's comment. Jonique was closer, just two desks away. The cornrows she had during track season were long gone. Now her hair hung in springy coils that brushed her cheeks when she moved. Her snug T-shirt and shorts revealed cords of toned muscle in her arms and legs. Compared to Jonique, Naveah was tall and lean, with almost no curves to speak of.

"You got the same build as me in high school," Mom always said. *"A distance runner's body."*

Naveah shrugged off her mother's words and noticed Jonique looking at her. For a second, their eyes locked, but then Jonique's gaze landed on Naveah's phone. The small screen glowed with Naveah's face, distorted by the dramatic makeup filter.

Jonique rolled her eyes and sucked her teeth.

Embarrassment spread over Naveah's cheeks, and her face suddenly felt on fire. On most days, Jonique acted as if Naveah was invisible. But during the rare times they did speak, Jonique always seemed bored and unimpressed, as if she was better than Naveah.

When I have thousands of followers, we'll see who's better, Naveah thought. She pictured a future when she had throngs of people on her pages, loving her posts and hanging on her every word, making her feel important.

Maybe millions, she thought. *Then we'll see who's—*

"Isn't that right, Naveah?" Ms. Sherman's voice cut through the air. Naveah flinched and realized the teacher was standing right behind her. How had she crossed the room so quickly?

"Uh..." Naveah stammered. She could feel her classmates' sudden stares, their eyes crawling over her. She wished she could be like Klassy Kay and think of something clever or funny to say. But her mind was blank. All that came out was a confused mutter. "Uh, yeah."

Ms. Sherman glanced into Naveah's lap. The heavily made-up Naveah still stared up from her phone screen.

"Give that to me, please." Ms. Sherman stretched out her hand.

"What?" Naveah's face seared. A few students whispered and another laughed. The classroom seemed to fill with the sound.

"You know the rules, Naveah. No phones in my class. If I see it, I take it," Ms. Sherman said sternly. Naveah knew she couldn't argue. The teacher had scolded her twice before in recent weeks. "C'mon, hand it over."

A mocking grunt cut the silence from where Jonique sat. Naveah looked back and noticed her smirking, but her eyes were aimed forward, as if she hadn't made a sound.

"Naveah?" Ms. Sherman's tone was as sharp as jagged glass. "*Now.*"

The classroom twittered with nervous laughter. Naveah wished a hole would open in the speckled tile floor and swallow her up. She reluctantly dropped the phone into the teacher's outstretched hand.

"That's your third strike, Naveah. It means I'll be contacting your parents—"

"Aww, come on, Ms. Sherm! It's the last week of school!" Kareem Burnett blurted from his seat two rows back. "Don't do her like that!"

Naveah winced. She couldn't believe that Kareem, the shy, chubby kid from her fourth-grade class who had morphed into an athlete this year, was suddenly trying to defend her.

"First off, Kareem, this has nothing to do with you, though I'm sure Naveah appreciates your concern." A few students snickered as Ms. Sherman shifted her gaze to Kareem and gave him a tight-lipped smile.

"I know, but…" Kareem shook his head so hard his twists brushed the dark brown skin of his forehead. "Man," he muttered. "That's just cold."

"Second," the teacher continued, turning back to Naveah. "The rules have been in place all year for a reason. As long as you are in my class, they still apply. That goes for everyone. Unless you'd rather discuss this with Principal Spencer, Naveah, you can pick up your phone from me at the end of the day. You understand?"

Nevaeh nodded, gritting her teeth and wishing the day, the school year, and the stupid class would end for good. When the bell finally rang, she bolted for the hallway.

"Remember to stop by after your last class to get your phone," Ms. Sherman called out to her, but Naveah didn't turn back. She couldn't stand to see Jonique's smirking face or hear what she might say next. Instead, Naveah took the far corridor to get to PE, her next class.

The path was longer but less crowded, and it also took her past Bluford High's trophy case just outside the gymnasium doors. She had visited the case many times this year. Besides trophies and assorted plaques, it contained framed pictures of past teams, retired coaches, and former champions.

They stared out at passing students from behind a sheet of protective plexiglass. Some of the photos were recent but most dated back many years, from when the school was still known as Woodrow Wilson High School, not Guion Bluford High. Naveah stopped in front of one familiar trophy that was taller than the others.

Etched in gold, the words *STATE CHAMPIONS* glimmered faintly. The trophy was twenty-five years old. Behind it, mounted on the wall, was a grainy color portrait of the winning girls track team. Naveah knew it well. Smiling back at her from the middle of the front row was her mother. Young and slender, she stood several inches taller than most of the other girls around her. Her hair was cut in a tiny afro, but her smile was wide—and unchanged. On her chest, two golden medals gleamed: one for the race she had won and one for the team's first-place victory. Mom still had the medals in a box in her bedroom closet. She shared them with Naveah last summer after she graduated eighth grade.

"Now it's your turn!" Mom had gushed with excitement over Naveah's starting high school. *"I know you're gonna get trophies one day. Maybe track or maybe something else. We'll see."*

But so far, Naveah's high school experience had been nothing like Mom's. Instead, it was quiet, dull, and often lonely. Back in grade school, she was part of a core group of friends that played soccer and basketball and went to birthday parties together. They sat at the same lunch tables and even had sleepovers sometimes. But in middle school, the group started drifting apart. Then, in seventh grade, Naveah hit a growth spurt that made her taller than most of her classmates. It felt awkward to be all legs, towering over everyone, yet almost completely flat up top. Some girls started getting boy crazy, and others formed new cliques. Naveah gradually stopped being included. She had hoped everything would change at Bluford. But now, at the end of her freshman year, it seemed worse. She was just too tall, too skinny, too quiet, too awkward, too… something.

Naveah instinctively reached for her phone only to remember it was missing.

The one companion that made her feel "normal" at school was the phone she got in sixth grade. It kept her company at lunch when no one joined her, and it filled her evenings when there wasn't anything better to do. The endless posts, videos, memes, and conversations made her feel connected.

With them, Naveah wasn't alone. Yet now Ms. Sherman had taken all that away.

"I'll be contacting your parents," the teacher had said.

Naveah dreaded the conversation she knew was coming. Mom already thought she was on the phone too much. She had nagged her about it a thousand times. What would she do after Ms. Sherman called?

Naveah gazed at Mom's picture. On days when she was lonely, she would study her, trying to draw comfort from her mother's smiling face, a secret no one else in the school seemed to know about. But as the year wore on, Mom's winning smile felt less and less reassuring. Some days, like right now, it seemed more like a reminder that she had little in common with her mother.

"We're not the same, Mom," Naveah whispered. "I'm nothing like you."

The late bell blared overhead as Naveah reached the gym locker room. She barely finished changing into her shorts and T-shirt before Ms. Gaskins, their stocky and freckle-faced gym teacher, blew her whistle and summoned the class for attendance.

"We're finishing the school year with a quick unit on track," the teacher announced, as Naveah rushed to join the group. At the mention of track, a chorus of groans filled their section of the gym. Ms. Gaskins ignored them and kept talking.

"We'll jog a couple of laps to get warmed up, and then we'll do some short sprints. Nothing too serious, but those of you who want to are welcome to do more."

"There is no way I'm doing that," muttered Alexis Newby, a girl Naveah had spoken to occasionally in class.

"And since we can't have our two track stars on the same team," Ms. Gaskins continued, "Malika and Jonique will be our captains. Let's split into two groups."

Ms. Gaskins began dividing up the class. Naveah breathed a sigh of relief when she was assigned to Malika.

The class lumbered out to the track and began a slow warm-up jog. Jonique and Malika were out in front leading them. Naveah noticed they moved effortlessly, talking the whole time, even as others in the class were already sweating and laboring to keep up.

"Okay!" Ms. Gaskins gestured them toward a chalk line on the track's coarse red surface. "Let's get a little competition going. Pair up. You're going to run half a lap—just 200 meters. See if you can beat the person next to you. Once you're done, walk around the rest of the track and get back in line. Understand?"

Girls mumbled nervously and some shook their heads, but Naveah felt an odd sense of excitement.

"What do we get if we beat everybody?" Jonique cut in from the front of the line.

"Bragging rights and a good word to Coach Sherman. Like you even need that," Ms. Gaskins replied with a knowing smile. "First pair, take your place."

Naveah joined the back of the line and looked around to see who she would be racing against. Up ahead, a whistle blew and Malika and Jonique, the first two runners, sprinted out onto the track. Even though Naveah could see they weren't running hard, they still moved with speed and power that was impossible not to notice. As they neared the finish line, they both slowed down and carefully stepped to the finish in unison. Their race was a tie.

"Next!" Ms. Gaskins barked.

Another pair of girls took off. Though they seemed to work harder, their speed looked to be about half that of the track stars. That was true of each group that followed until a pair of girls who were close friends decided not to race at all and simply walked around the track. As she waited for them to finish, Naveah considered walking too, but no one seemed to want to go with her. She let other pairs go ahead of her until only a few students remained who hadn't run. Should she just walk alone? Naveah took her place at the starting line, but no one joined her in the other lane.

"Who's next?" Ms. Gaskins called when she realized the spot was empty. "C'mon, someone go with her." No one stepped up at first, but then Naveah recognized a muscled form step into the starting area.

"I'll go," Jonique offered. She eyed Naveah like a cat sizing up a fat mouse.

"But you already ran," Ms. Gaskins noted.

"I don't mind going again," Jonique cooed. "It's fine."

A hush swept over the remaining students. Did Jonique want to race her? Is that what was happening? Naveah wondered. Part of her was ready to walk around the track and not even try. No one would even care. A race in gym class was meaningless. But another part of her remembered the race in middle school and was suddenly hungry for a repeat.

Jonique seemed to remember too. She took her position in the lane next to Naveah's. Concentration furrowed her face as she toed the line and readied for the start. Naveah felt her determination to win fill the air between them like the electric charge before a storm. It might have choked her—frozen her limbs so she was too scared to move—had it not been for the memory of seventh grade.

I beat you then, Naveah thought. *What if I can do it again?*

Malika stood on the edge of the track watching them. Alexis did too.

Ms. Gaskin blew her whistle.

Naveah watched as Jonique exploded into movement at an impossible speed. Already several feet behind, Naveah swung her arms and took off. Her shoes scraped and clawed against the track as she accelerated. She stretched her legs into fast strides and pumped her arms. Seconds into the race, she lifted her head and focused on Jonique's back, which was already about ten feet out in front of her. How was she so quick?

Naveah pushed harder, dug deeper. The pat-pat-pat of her feet pounded against the track like drums. Suddenly there were other noises in the background too—someone was screaming something—but Naveah didn't try to understand what they were saying. She concentrated on Jonique's back as it grew larger. Inch by inch, step by step, Naveah watched the space between them close.

Ten feet melted into eight…

Then dissolved into six...
And shrank down to four...

Ms. Gaskins blew her whistle as they reached the finish line. Jonique had clearly won, but Naveah had closed the gap. She had gained ground on the champion. Naveah slowed to a walk, panting, her heart thumping wildly in her chest.

"That was amazing! Good race, girls. That's what competition does!" Ms. Gaskins yelled to the class. "You don't know what you can do until you're pressed. Good job!"

Naveah closed her eyes and put her hands on her hips. The sun was warm, but a slight breeze cooled her sweaty skin. Somehow, she felt stronger and more powerful than she had moments ago. She hadn't won, but maybe she could have if the race had been longer? Maybe?

"You know I just smoked you, right?" Jonique cut in, shattering her thoughts. "Only reason you got close is 'cause I let you. I was walking at the end. Remember that."

Jonique jogged off to join Malika and the rest of class. Naveah's mind kept spinning with what had just happened.

No matter what Jonique said, she felt as though she could have beaten her if she had a better start or another ten meters to run. Maybe it could have been seventh grade all over again. Maybe she *was* her mother's daughter?

Naveah imagined posting her thoughts on her phone once she got it back. The idea made her fingers twitch with excitement.

Chapter 2

"Can I have my phone back?" Naveah asked at the end of the day.

She had been trying to remain patient, nodding along and biting her tongue in the front row of Ms. Sherman's classroom as the teacher lectured her.

"Lack of focus…highly distractible…constantly on your phone." The teacher droned on until Naveah could barely sit still.

"I get it, and I'll do better," she huffed. "Now can I please have it back?"

"Naveah," the teacher sighed, "this is important. I've been watching you all year, and it doesn't seem as if you've found your place at Bluford yet. Maybe you could try joining a club? Or going out for a sport next year? Come to cross country this fall or track next spring. I'm serious. I know social media is fun, but you're missing out on so much."

Missing out? Naveah struggled not to roll her eyes. *You don't get it*, she wanted to say.

"I'm sorry, but I have to meet my little brother at the bus stop. If I'm late, he'll be all alone," she said instead, knowing it wasn't completely true. Christian was eight and could walk the short distance from the bus stop to their house by himself.

Ms. Sherman exhaled wearily and placed the phone into Naveah's outstretched hand as if it pained her to do so. Notifications flashed across the tiny screen. Naveah's fingers itched to unlock it and start scrolling, but first she had to get away from the teacher.

"Thanks," she said, trying not to seem too eager. "I'll think about what you said for next year—"

"I hope so, Naveah, for your sake," Ms. Sherman replied, sounding unconvinced. "By the way, I sent your mother a text about what happened today. She hasn't answered yet, but I'm sure she will."

Naveah shrugged as if Ms. Sherman's news was unimportant, yet she knew there would be trouble the second Mom read the text. Hiding her thoughts, Naveah rushed out of the school, eager to watch the rest of Klassy Kay's video and forget all about Ms. Sherman. She could try copying Klassy's style with the filter that gave her thick eyelashes and flawless skin. Or maybe she would make a post about what happened on the track earlier in the day.

What should I say? she wondered.

"Naveah!" a rough voice called out. She looked up to see Kareem emerging from the high school behind her carrying a gym bag. He was nothing like the short kid with the inhaler who sat out of Mr. Matthews's fourth grade gym class every other day. Now he was her height and muscular. But why was he suddenly calling her name, she wondered.

"Did Sherm give back your phone?"

"Yeah, I just got it," she answered, waiving it for a second. "She didn't make it easy."

"She gave you one of them long talks, didn't she? That's a Sherman sermon."

"A what?" Naveah smiled, trying to hide how awkward she felt speaking with him. "That's exactly what it was. How'd you know?"

"She gives them all the time when she's coaching. That's just how she gets when she cares about something," Kareem added, shifting his gym bag to his other shoulder.

Naveah tried to fight off a wave of shyness. "Thanks for what you said in class today."

"It's all good," Kareem replied. "I know how she is. She didn't call your mom, did she?"

Naveah nodded grimly. "She texted her."

"For real? That's just extra. We all on our phones! Is she tryna ruin your summer by makin' your parents crazy?"

"Too late. They already crazy, especially my mom," Naveah admitted, wondering why Kareem was suddenly so talkative. "She's gonna nag me all summer after this. But I'm not gonna lie—she'd probably do that anyway about something else. She always finds a reason."

"If it makes you feel any better, my mom's the same way," Kareem admitted. "I'm just gonna avoid her this summer by working out. I'm training for football tryouts in August."

"Are you serious?" Naveah asked, unable to hide the surprise in her voice.

"I know. Not what you expected from that chubby kid with asthma, right?"

"No, that's not what I meant," she replied quickly, trying to find some way to make the moment less awkward. "It's just...I didn't know you liked football," she added.

Kareem grinned. "Well...now you know. When I was little, I was too sick to play. Now that I'm better, it feels like time to get off the sidelines." He seemed to be studying her reaction.

Naveah wished she could think of something clever or funny to say, but she just wasn't used to talking, especially to boys. Seconds passed and the silence made her cringe inside.

"So…I gotta meet my little brother at his bus stop," she added finally, eager to escape yet happy that he had stopped to talk to her.

"Yeah, no. Me, too. I mean, I gotta go too," he said finally, looking sheepish.

They walked away from the high school together, the silence broken only by the swoosh of passing traffic. Naveah tried to imagine what Klassy Kay would do in this moment, but the only thing that came to mind was to take a selfie, and that didn't seem right. She glanced at Kareem. He sighed, stammered, and shifted his eyes, as if he was nervous too.

"So…see you this summer sometime?"

"Definitely," he replied.

Naveah clutched her phone and fought the urge to sprint all the way home.

Naveah was surprised to see Mom's black Honda Accord parked in front of their townhouse. Usually, Mom didn't get home from the daycare center until at least 6:00 p.m.

Why is Mom home so early? she wondered. Then she remembered Ms. Sherman's text, and her stomach sank. Had Mom come home early to punish her? Naveah took a deep breath and braced herself before stepping inside.

The TV was on in the living room. Christian sat on the floor directly in front of it, a worn Xbox controller in his hands. Even though he could only have been home for a short time, he was already lost in his favorite game, Minecraft. He and Naveah used to play together before she started high school. He once named their country Chriveah, a combination of their names, and it stuck. Together, they built villages and farms and a stone bridge that crossed a river and connected their two sections.

"Hey," she said, watching him plant digital carrots in a field. "Where's Mom?"

Christian nodded his head toward the bathroom.

"Did she seem mad when you saw her?"

"I dunno." Christian shrugged as he began adding a field of pumpkins next to his carrots. "She was in there when I got here." He paused to scroll through an on-screen tool menu and selected a shovel. "Why would she be mad?"

"No reason." Naveah shrugged, staring down the hallway. She was certain Mom had gotten Ms. Sherman's text and raced home early to deal with her.

"You did something again, didn't you?" Christian asked, looking up from his game. "Why are you and Mom always arguing?"

"I didn't do anything, okay," Naveah huffed. "This is none of your business."

The bathroom door suddenly creaked open, and Mom stepped into the hall. Framed by the dark doorway, she seemed unrelated to the slender teenager with the radiant smile in Bluford's trophy case. The decades had made her face rounder and her shoulders broader. Still tall, she was now heavy in her torso and midsection. Mom's skin had changed, too: getting thinner and blotchier with age. Her once playful brown eyes were far more serious, and they flashed whenever she was angry. Naveah could see the fire in them now as Mom raised her hand, showing Naveah her phone with a long text message on it.

"What's this mess about you having your phone taken away at school?"

"It wasn't a big deal—" Naveah began.

"Oh, it's a big deal, all right," Mom snapped. "You know better, Naveah. We don't send you to school to study Snapchat. It's bad enough that you're on your phone all the time here at home. But at school too? That's not happening."

"It's the last week of school, Mom!" Naveah protested. "I didn't think that she—"

"That's right—you didn't think. All you seem to care about is taking selfies and following a bunch of fake people pretending to be things they ain't. And it keeps you from doing real things right in front of you. Like schoolwork or making friends or enjoying high school!" Mom pressed her hand to her stomach and winced as if the conversation was hurting her. "I don't understand you, Naveah. Back when I was in school—"

"Please don't go there again," Naveah muttered. The last thing she wanted to hear was Mom boast about the good old days before phones when she was a popular school athlete. It only made Naveah feel worse. "It won't happen again. I promise."

"It certainly won't happen again, Naveah, that's for sure," Mom grumbled, stepping closer but still rubbing her stomach. Her motion was heavy and plodding, and dark rings of weariness hung beneath her eyes. She kept one hand on her abdomen but stretched the other towards Naveah. "It won't happen again because you just lost the privilege," she said, nodding toward the phone. "Give it to me."

"Come on, Mom!" Naveah cried. "It's the end of the year. None of the other teachers even care—"

"That phone's been practically glued to your hand all year. We hardly see your face anymore without a screen in front of it. And all those hours you spend tryin' to imitate those people you follow!" She shook her head. "It's got to stop. Right *now*. You need to find something else to do with yourself!"

"Okay, okay," Naveah said, clutching her phone tightly. "I'll join a club next year. I promise—"

"Fine. But you're gonna give me that phone right now."

"Wait! For how long?"

"Until I see some changes," Mom said, then snapped her fingers. "And I'm gonna help you start makin' 'em. Maybe if you weren't always on that phone, you'd have some real friends. We didn't have phones when I was in school, and you know what we did? Joined clubs. Played sports. When I was on the track team…"

Not again, Naveah thought to herself. Not more proof that Mom was great and that she was a nobody. A disappointment. Naveah couldn't stand it.

"…they used to call me 'Lightning'," Mom went on. "That's how fast I used to be—"

"Used to be," Naveah muttered, unable to hold back her frustration. "Back in the olden days. You say it all the time!"

"Watch your mouth!" Mom said sharply. "I'm not feeling so good today, and I am definitely not in the mood for this crap from you! Now hand it over."

"No!" Naveah snapped, alarmed at her own voice. She knew it was too loud, too harsh—wrong. She had never spoken to Mom this way, and she didn't want to now. But something inside her wouldn't let her back down. Not after the day she had, the year she had. Not after Ms. Sherman's lecture and Mom's constant nagging. It was all too much.

"Naveah! Give me your phone right now." Mom lunged forward and grabbed Naveah's hand.

"No!" Naveah twisted away, bumping her hip against Mom's stomach.

An awful groan sliced the air. Naveah turned to see her mother double over, gripping her midsection. Then Mom's legs buckled, and she collapsed to the floor, moaning with pain. Naveah froze in shock.

"Mom!" Christian raced in from the living room and rushed to his mother's side. "What did you do?" he screamed at Naveah.

"Nothing. I just bumped her. I didn't mean it—"

"You hurt her. Why did you do that?"

Naveah felt strangely detached, as though she was watching everything happen on a screen, yet it was all right in front of her. Mom lay crumpled at her feet breathing heavily. Beads of sweat dotted her forehead. Her hand pressed tight against her belly. Naveah knelt beside her, unsure what to do.

"Are you okay?" she asked, gently touching her mother's back. "What should I do?"

Mom gave a slight nod. "I told you. I'm not feeling too good today," she panted. "I think…" She moaned again, and her voice turned into an awful wail that filled the room.

"Mom!" Christian cried, panic in his eyes. *"Naveah, do something!"*

Her hands trembling with panic, Naveah used her phone to dial 9-1-1.

Mom in with doctors now. Running tests.

Naveah reread her father's text over and over, searching for answers. Nearly two hours had passed since the paramedics had barged into their house and taken Mom away in a blur of sirens and chaos. Dad had gone straight from the Amazon shipping center where he worked to the hospital to join Mom. Though he promised to send updates, he had sent only one so far, and that was an hour ago. Since then, their townhouse had been eerily quiet, as if it too was waiting for news.

What's taking so long? Naveah wanted to know. She had already texted Dad the question twice, but he never answered.

Stay here with Christian were Mom's last words as the medics wheeled her out.

Naveah tried to listen and keep an eye on Christian, but he was already back on Minecraft, making odd changes to Chriveah and hardly speaking to her. She watched in silence as he began to take apart the old stone bridge they had once built together. Since the paramedics left, he had also set fire to his new orchard, leaving the area bleak and barren. Yet she was relieved he at least had the game to distract him from worrying.

"I'm sure she's gonna be fine," Naveah said at one point as he built a wall across a road that connected his portion or his Minecraft world to hers. "You know how tough Mom is."

Christian grunted. His fingers worked feverishly on the controller. His eyes were pink and bloodshot, but he didn't blink.

"You shouldn't have pushed her," he said finally, his gaze locked on the screen. "She was fine until you did that."

His words hit like a punch in her stomach. Naveah slumped on the sofa next to him and stared at the floor where Mom had fallen.

"I didn't mean to," she admitted, grabbing the other controller to join him. "I was just upset, and it all happened so fast. I would never hurt Mom."

"But you did," Christian grumbled, glaring at her. His eyes were glassy but angry too. He dropped his controller and stormed out of the living room. A second later, Naveah heard the thud of his bedroom door closing. She was alone.

It's your fault, the silence seemed to say. *You are the reason Mom got hurt.* Christian had said it too. And in the heavy quiet of the lonely living room, Naveah couldn't escape the voices in her own mind that echoed those words.

If you hadn't disappointed her.
If you hadn't yelled at her.
If you hadn't pushed her.

Images of Mom writhing in pain flashed like lightning in Naveah's mind. Unable to shake them, she grabbed her phone and began scrolling, anything to fill the silence and stop herself from thinking.

Her TikTok feed answered with an endless spool of cat videos and silly dances, gross-looking smoothie recipes and random school fights, fashion tips and style updates, and an army of influencers with perfect skin and flawless bodies that Naveah wished she could have. Soon Naveah could feel her thoughts calming, her mind numbing, the minutes passing, her eyes growing heavy until…

Naveah felt someone shaking her shoulder.

"C'mon, Naveah. Go to bed."

Naveah opened her eyes to see her father standing over her. He was wearing his brown delivery uniform. She glanced at her phone. It was 10:53 p.m. The events of the day flooded back into her mind as she realized she had fallen asleep on the sofa. When had he gotten home? What happened to Mom? A million questions suddenly swept over her.

"Where's Mom?" she asked, sitting up.

"Yeah, where is she?" Christian appeared in his pajamas at the end of the hallway. He squinted against the living room lights.

Dad sighed and rubbed his own eyes. He seemed as if he had aged several years since Naveah had seen him that morning. "They're keeping her for a couple days so she can recover, and they can run some more tests," he said, pausing strangely. "She'll be home Saturday."

"Recover?" Naveah repeated. Had she hurt Mom that much? "What's wrong with her?"

"Is Mom okay?" Christian added, fidgeting with his hands.

"She's better now than when I got to the hospital," Dad said quickly, turning away as he spoke. "She had to have her appendix removed. Doctors said it was starting to burst. That's what caused her all that pain," he explained. "She's lucky she got to the hospital when she did or else it could have been worse. She's pretty tired right now, but she's already starting to feel better. Your mom's a fighter. I don't need more tests to tell me that."

A wave of relief washed over Naveah. Yet as she watched her father's face, she noticed the way he spoke didn't quite match his words. It was as if an invisible weight hung on his words and held them down. He glanced at his phone for a second, read a text, and sighed.

"Why is she having more tests?" Naveah asked. The question lingered in the air for a few seconds before Dad finally replied.

"It's nothing to worry about, Naveah," Dad added quickly. "Just the doctors being extra careful, that's all."

Again, his words made sense, but his voice sounded artificial somehow, like the narrators she sometimes heard on TikTok.

"C'mon, it's late, you two. I'm exhausted. Go to bed. You'll see Mom Saturday morning. You can talk all you want then." Dad ushered Christian to his room and then retreated to his own bedroom without another word.

Chapter 3

On way with mom.

Dad's text flashed on Naveah's phone late Saturday morning.

Like all his answers to her questions about Mom, his text seemed short and distant, almost as if it pained him to say anything about her.

Was he angry about the cell phone argument she had with Mom? Naveah almost wished he was. At least there would be something to talk about. Instead, he had become a tight-lipped stranger ever since Mom went to the hospital. Last night, when she had asked about visiting Mom there with Christian, Dad refused outright.

"No," he huffed, shaking his head and dropping a $20 bill on the table for her to buy pizza for dinner. "That hospital is no place for kids. Besides, Mom's tired from all the tests and doctors fussing over her. Let her rest. You guys can see her when she comes home."

Dad didn't return from the hospital until late last night. Naveah had heard his keys jingling in the front doorway past midnight, and then she heard him leave again this morning just as the sun was peeking through the blinds of her bedroom. His behavior planted a nervous knot in Naveah's stomach, one that twinged when she heard Dad's CRV suddenly pull up outside.

"They're here," Naveah announced, shoving her phone into the pocket of her sweatpants.

Christian tossed aside the Xbox controller and raced out the door in his socks. Mom rose heavily from the passenger seat. Dad hovered next to her as if she were made of glass and could shatter into a thousand pieces if she were to fall. Without warning, Christian darted to Mom's midsection and threw his arms around her.

Mom winced in pain.

"Easy, Chris!" Dad warned, trying to nudge him back, but Mom waved him off and squeezed Christian back.

"It's okay. It's okay. I missed you too, baby," she said, rubbing his back.

Watching them, Naveah felt a wave of shame for what had happened. She wished she had just handed the phone over when Mom first asked for it. "I'm sorry," she said finally, barely able to look at her mother. "I didn't mean to—"

"It's okay," Mom murmured in her ear, hugging her. Mom's breath felt like a soft feather. "I used to be a teenager too. I know how hard it is. Still, let's not do this again, y'hear me?" she said, rubbing her back.

Naveah nodded and closed her eyes. For a moment, she was a little girl again, nestled safe in her mother's arms. But when Mom gently let go, Naveah noticed her father. He looked tired and sad. His eyes almost seemed to glisten.

"C'mon, let's go inside," Dad urged. "It's been a long couple of days."

"Amen!" Mom replied, smiling weakly.

Her father took Mom's arm and tried to lead her inside, but she waved his hand away.

"Would you stop treating me like that? I can walk. See?" She then rushed awkwardly toward the house, nearly tripping at one point. When she reached the front step, she winced and trembled as she forced her body up the stairs, finally leaning on Dad for support on the top step.

"What happened, Mom?" Christian asked, watching her struggle.

"I'm just a little sore, that's all. The operation took something out of me," she explained. Once inside, Mom ignored Dad's suggestion that she go to her room and refused his request that she sit down and rest. Instead, she headed straight for the kitchen and started opening up cabinets.

"I'ma make us a nice brunch, and you're gonna help me," she said to Christian as she scanned the refrigerator.

"Are you sure?" he asked.

"Yes, I'm sure," she huffed. "All I've done for two days is sit in bed and eat nasty hospital food. I need to do something, but I'ma need you to help me. Can you do that?"

Christian nodded. Naveah noticed her dad shaking his head and rubbing his temples as if he suddenly had a bad headache.

"C'mon, Amaya. You heard what the doctors said," Dad pleaded. "You need to be careful—"

"I'll be careful, Julius," Mom snapped, but then her face softened. "Christian and Naveah will make sure of it, but I gotta do this, okay?" Mom's eyes flashed with determination. Dad sighed and nodded reluctantly.

"Naveah, grab eggs and butter. Christian, get me a big bowl," Mom instructed.

Naveah felt trapped between her mother's orders and the pained look on her father's face. She handed Mom the eggs just as Christian placed a blue mixing bowl in front of her. Dad crossed his arms. Tension filled the air like smog over the city. Naveah couldn't stand it.

"Guys, what's happening?" she asked finally.

Mom's back stiffened, but she didn't speak. For a long moment, the only sound was the wet crack of eggs smacking against the bowl.

"Amaya, please," Dad said in a low voice. "We can't keep this a secret. Remember what you said. We talked about this."

Mom took a deep breath and nodded slowly. "You're right. You kids need to know what's what. It's not fair to keep you guessing."

Naveah waited as her mother grabbed a fork and began scrambling the eggs in the bowl. Her brow furrowed as she worked, as if the effort required all her strength and concentration. They all watched as she slid the frying pan to the closest burner and turned on the stove. A blue gas flame hissed to life as Mom dropped a pat of butter into the pan and watched it melt. She then poured the eggs into the pan. They hissed and bubbled back at her.

"Know *what?*" Naveah asked, unable to wait any longer. "What's going on?"

Mom clenched her jaw but kept working. With one hand, she stirred the black pan with a spoon. With the other, she sprinkled in a handful of cheese and then a dash of salt. For a long minute, she cooked in silence before switching off the stove, grabbing the pan by its handle, and turning toward them.

"Well, when they removed my appendix, they found a shadow on my X-ray."

"A shadow?" Christian repeated. The word seemed ominous.

"What's that mean?" Naveah asked.

"Well," Mom said matter-of-factly, spooning scrambled eggs onto each plate. "I took a bunch of tests, and it turns out I have pancreatic cancer."

Her words hit like a bomb blast. Dad slumped. Christian's face twisted in confusion. An icy shiver crept down Naveah's back.

Cancer.

Naveah shuddered. A rush of awful images flooded through her mind. Frail people connected to machines or losing their hair—or worse.

"But they can fix it? Right, Mom?" Christian asked, his voice strained with worry. "They got medicine, right? Or an operation?"

"It's not really something that they can operate on, baby," Mom explained. She set the pan back on the stove and slumped in her chair, resting her hands on her midsection. "But there are some treatments we can try…" she stammered and glanced at Dad.

He reached over and covered her fingers with his own, squeezing them gently.

"Even though the doctors say the cancer is spreading," she continued. "They say it has metastasized—that's just a fancy word for 'gotten aggressive.' But I can be aggressive, too," Mom insisted in a bright voice. "I'm going to fight it with everything I've got. Starting soon, I'll be doing chemo and radiation treatments at the hospital three times every week. We gotta go hard if I'm gonna beat it. And I *am* gonna beat it. That's all there is to *that*. So, I don't want to hear any crying and I don't want to see no sad faces. We're fine. I'm fine. It's fine. Got it?"

She locked eyes on each one of them as if her stare alone would convince them that her words were true. Naveah noticed Christian seemed satisfied with her explanation.

"Okay, Mom." He smiled and nodded.

Yet Naveah struggled in her mother's gaze. The words "chemo" and "radiation" echoed in her mind. An image of Mom as a sick and withered version of herself haunted her thoughts for a moment. Yet it seemed so unlikely. Mom was too strong, too big, too stubborn. Naveah had never seen her back away from any kind of fight. If anyone could beat cancer, it was her. Right?

"Got it," Naveah replied, trying to sound positive and upbeat, almost like Klassy Kay when she live streamed.

Mom eyed her as if she recognized Klassy's tone and didn't quite approve.

"This...this is gonna be tough, guys," Dad cautioned, rubbing Mom's back. "For your mother. For all of us." His voice wavered slightly, and he paused to clear his throat before continuing. "There's gonna be lots of trips to the hospital and days when your mother won't feel good. We all gonna have to pull together to help. I'll be changing my work schedule so I can be around more during the day, and you kids will need to step up with chores or whatever Mom asks. You got that?"

Naveah and Christian nodded as Dad wiped something from his eye. Together they ate their eggs in silence, pretending everything was the same as before Mom said the words "pancreatic cancer."

After brunch, Naveah escaped to her bedroom and closed the door. She sat down on the edge of her bed and pulled out her phone, her fingers itchy to find out more.

Pancreatic cancer.

The words rattled in her mind like dice in a cup. Her parents had made it sound as if everything was all right—and that probably meant it wasn't, Naveah concluded.

She googled the words, and an endless list of links appeared. One was from a big-name hospital she had heard of. She took a deep breath and tapped on it. Her phone lit up with text.

> The pancreas is a gland behind the stomach. It produces chemicals that break down food….

Naveah scrolled with her thumb, her eyes scanning the paragraphs looking for answers.

> Pancreatic cancer has no symptoms early on….It is often found too late for surgery.

She remembered Mom saying her cancer couldn't be operated on. That was why she was getting radiation. She skimmed further, looking for something positive. The word "palliative" wasn't one she knew, but it appeared in the treatment section, so she scrolled to it.

> Palliative care is care given to patients to ease pain before death….

Naveah's heart sank to her stomach. She dropped her phone as if it had bitten her.

No, she thought. There wasn't any reason to talk about death, was there?

Naveah's bedroom suddenly felt like it was spinning. Her palms grew cold and clammy. She picked up the phone and did a new search for the other word Mom had used to describe her illness.

Metastic or something, she recalled. Naveah wasn't sure how to spell it, but autocorrect took over, and soon her phone pulled results for "metastasized pancreatic cancer."

She discovered right away that "metastasized" meant "spread." Mom's cancer had spread to different parts of her body. Naveah felt the blood drain from her hands.

> Once the cancer metastasizes to other parts of the body, most pancreatic cancer patients live less than a year….

It was too much to take in. How could it be true? Aside from her illness the other day, Mom seemed as strong and tough as ever. The article had to be wrong, Naveah decided. It knew nothing about Mom or how much of a fighter she was. Maybe it was fake too. Fake news, like people were always saying about the internet. Naveah clung to this idea like a lifeline.

Buzz!

Her phone suddenly vibrated with notifications. A post on Instagram was getting lots of views from people she followed. Grateful for the distraction, Naveah opened the app, surprised that she recognized the background in the shaky video.

The girls in gym shorts, the familiar bleachers, and the gritty red track were all unmistakable. It was Bluford High.

The clip went in and out of focus before locking in on two girls racing. A muscular girl with thick brown legs streaked into the frame. Her arms were bent into sharp angles and pumping like pistons as she sprinted around the curve of the track. She seemed to be going impossibly fast—too fast to catch—until another girl appeared in the frame. This girl was taller and more slender, and her long strides gobbled up the track's coarse surface with every step. Her eyes were locked on the girl in front of her with a fierce determination that seemed to eclipse everything else. She sped around the track until she was only feet away from the first girl when they crossed the finish line. She ran so hard she didn't seem to notice the hoots and cheers of classmates erupting at the finish.

Naveah blinked in surprise. Of course, the first girl was Jonique, but that second girl burning down the track was her! Someone had snuck a phone onto the track and recorded their race from last week's gym class.

There were three comments on the video too. Two were almost identical:

> That girl's fast as lightning! ⚡⚡⚡
> Get it, long legs!

But the last one hit like a slap:

> She looks like a skeleton tryin' to dance 💀💀💀💀💀

Maybe it was the news about Mom's condition, or all the scary information she had just read, but suddenly Naveah snapped. Fury and outrage boiled in her chest. Who would say such a mean thing about her? Naveah looked at the name of the person who posted the comment: JoniQuEEN11.

It was Jonique! Naveah was sure of it.

"I coulda beat you!" she yelled at the phone, as if Jonique could hear. With shaking fingers Naveah typed a response:

Next time 😳

She hit "send," her heart pounding and her breath coming fast as if she was circling the track all over again. For a moment, it felt good to have answered Jonique on the post, but then a reply appeared under her comment.

Name the date, girl. It was from JoniQuEEN11. A second later, another appeared.

Unless you scared.

Rage flared and bubbled in Naveah's chest and coursed through her fingertips. She had ignored Jonique's rudeness all year, but for some reason, she couldn't do it anymore. Rather than walk away, Naveah wanted to race her right now.

Tomorrow, she wanted to answer, but before she could reply, Jonique posted again.

This time it was the image of the leaderboard from last month's All City competition. Jonique's name was posted first under the mile winners with a time of 5 minutes, 47 seconds.

5:47 to go around the track four times?

Naveah had barely gone around it once, and it had taken everything she had to catch up to the girl. How could she possibly beat her?

"Naveah!" Mom called out. "Get off your phone and help your brother straighten up this kitchen. I'm supposed to be taking it easy."

"One minute," Naveah yelled back, her fingers twitching to respond.

"Not one minute. *Now*. Let's not do this again, Naveah."

Feeling a stab of guilt, Naveah quit the app and stormed out of her bedroom, unable to shake Jonique's last words.

Unless you scared.

Chapter 4

She a coward.

Daddy longlegs don't wanna get stomped.

She'd get smoked out there.

Naveah's pulse throbbed in her temples as she scrolled through the comments from her pew in the back of Holy Faith Church. By Sunday morning, it seemed as though almost everyone at Bluford had something to say. Even strangers and people she didn't know from school were commenting. Not all of them were negative, and some didn't seem to notice Jonique's challenge.

A good race!

They both fast. 🏃💨

Need a rematch.

Naveah wanted to reply last night. But after washing the dishes, wiping the counters, and taking out the trash, she added dusting and vacuuming to her chores to stop

Mom from working. It seemed her mother's first response to cancer was to clean, as if it could help drive away the disease somehow.

"Gotta get these chores done while we can," Mom had declared, stiffly moving from room to room, directing what needed to be done, while Dad hovered nearby.

"We got to support her and make sure she doesn't overdo it," Dad explained to Naveah a few times, though he too seemed exhausted.

After the chores were done, her parents insisted that they spend "family time" watching TV together, though Naveah wanted to flee to her room to check her phone. Mom became worse than Ms. Sherman, demanding that Naveah shut it off so they could watch some childish movie about a kid with superpowers. Only Christian seemed interested, but Naveah didn't dare say that.

"It's not gonna hurt either of you to unplug for a few hours. Nothing on your devices is more important than family," Mom said. She spoke with such seriousness that Naveah knew not to argue, especially not with Dad following her every move.

Yet it all felt fake to Naveah. They were acting as if everything was normal. Just another family night. The reality was that cancer had invaded their home, and everything was suddenly different. Mom was extra bossy. Dad seemed distant and defeated, and no one knew what to do or say or what might happen next. Stuck without her phone for distraction, Naveah felt trapped, as if she needed to run but was unable to move.

"Put on something nice. Your mother wants us to go to church as a family." Dad declared Sunday morning.

An hour later, Naveah sat in the pew behind her parents at Holy Faith Church, glancing at her phone during Reverend Mumford's never-ending sermon. She scrolled through her feed, eager to see what she had missed the night before.

...A split between a popular rapper and her NBA player boyfriend. Everyone seemed to criticize the couple as if they knew them personally. Some people were so mean that Naveah skipped their comments, especially in church.

...A cat with a body camera chasing a dog down the street.

...A dance move challenge along with thousands of attempts that were hilariously awful.

...A post from Klassy Kay about an expensive new line of lipstick.

Naveah swiped through them all and went back to the video of herself racing

Jonique. She watched it again and again. She really had almost beaten her—it seemed even closer than she had realized while she was running it.

Naveah revisited the comments too. Jonique's burned in her memory.

Unless you scared.

There were new responses. A stranger making fun of her skinny legs, a friend of Jonique's talking about how scared she was, others saying she'd get beat. One from KareemdaDream345 said: 🔥 🔥 🔥 Can we get a rematch?

But beneath them all was a new post from Jonique.

Told y'all she was scared.

A fresh wave of anger rose through the floor of the church, making Naveah's face burn.

Jonique was popular. And she was a champion. Naveah knew it made no sense to race her. There was no way she could run that fast. And yet—

Naveah felt a sharp nudge in her side. She looked up to see Christian who pointed quickly to Dad, who was scowling at her and her phone from his pew.

Put that away. He mouthed the words so clearly that she could hear them in her mind even though he was silent. Naveah shoved her phone in her pocket, struggling to sit still as Reverend Mumford talked about the power of faith.

When the congregation rose and began to sing, Naveah hastily opened her hymnal and stood up with them. She studied her parents who seemed too close to her and yet farther away than ever. She expected them to be glaring at her, but they weren't even looking. They were holding hands with tears on their faces. The sight of them hit like a knife to her heart. They seemed like different people from just days ago. So much had changed so quickly.

How much more is going to change? Naveah wondered.

Again, she fought the urge to get away, to bolt out the door, to run.

The early summer sun was scorching the streets after church, but Naveah didn't care. The sermon, the comments, the cancer articles, Mom and Dad's whispery conversations were all too much.

Rushing to her room, Naveah threw on some gym clothes, grabbed her Nikes, and headed outside. A hot breeze seemed to call to her and coax her forward. With no goal or destination, she leaned forward. Her shoes dug into the sidewalk as she took her first stride and launched. For a second, she imagined herself on the track again with Jonique up ahead, taunting her.

Coward.

The word was like the shot of a starter gun. Naveah began to push.

Inhale. Stride. Accelerate.

Her muscles answered her command, speeding her body down the street almost effortlessly, as if it were what she was meant to do. She could feel her pulse quicken as the first city block disappeared behind her. Soon her legs and arms fell into a powerful rhythm. It felt good to move, she realized, to be taken someplace by her body, not her phone.

"Slow down, baby, this is a residential street," someone yelled as she blew by.

"Go get it, girl," said another.

Naveah wove through the streets, ignoring the comments, the neighborhood traffic, and the sweat that gathered between her shoulder blades and stung her eyes as it rolled down her face.

Dogs barked around her. Car stereos blasted. Sirens howled. Trucks rumbled. The city breathed. Naveah ran through it all.

Block after block, she dashed through Jonique's meanness, blew past Ms. Sherman's disapproval, her awkwardness with

Kareem, and her constant arguments with Mom. Everything suddenly seemed smaller as she ran, melting away with each block she covered.

Her heartbeat raced as Naveah pushed harder, running to escape something far scarier than Jonique, something that made her want to run away the moment Mom said the word.

Cancer.

Naveah sprinted as fast as she could go, her thighs and calves burning, her arms swinging, her pulse a throbbing drum in her neck and ears. Without thinking, she had made a great looping circle through her neighborhood and approached a familiar sign.

> Welcome to Bluford High School
> Home of the Buccaneers

Sweat pouring down, her vision stinging and blurry, her lungs on fire, Naveah rocketed onto the empty track and dashed until her legs were weak and rubbery and could go no further. Alone in the long shadows of the late afternoon sun, Naveah slowed to a walk at the 400-meter finish line, breathless and disoriented.

Mom's cancer was still there. Everything she had run from still existed. But for a time, on the run, she had escaped them.

"Where were you?" Mom asked when Naveah returned home exhausted but strangely calm. "Your father was looking for you."

"I was out running."

Mom's eyes widened as an odd smile lit up her face.

Naveah could feel her watching as she raced to her bedroom and closed the door.

Hours later, while her parents were busy talking about bills, upcoming doctor visits, and work schedules, Naveah snuck her phone under the covers so the light could not be seen under her closed door.

"How are we gonna pay for this house when I stop working?" Mom was asking. "You know how much this treatment is gonna cost?"

"Amaya, we got more important things to worry about now, okay?" Dad answered.

"More important than a roof over our heads? I'ma work as long as I can."

"But it's your health, baby," Dad kept saying. "We gotta focus on that."

Naveah put in her earbuds so she didn't have to listen. Instead, she replayed the video of her race with Jonique. She studied how Jonique's fast start helped her surge to a quick lead and then focused on the transition where she started to gain on her. With her earbuds in, she could hear people in the crowd and even recognize a few voices from class. She turned up the volume and listened to the mix of laughter and cheers for Jonique.

Then she heard an exchange.

"That awkward girl is really fast," said someone in the crowd.

"She is! We totally need her on our team next year," came a distinctive reply as the video cut off. Naveah was almost certain it was Malika, the short-distance champion on Bluford's varsity team. She had been there the day of the race.

Naveah reread the comments again, pulling up the one that bothered her the most, the one she had been itching to answer ever since she had first discovered it.

Name the date, girl. Unless you scared.

Naveah finally tapped the box to reply.

On another day, she probably would have ignored it or blocked it or pretended it was all a joke. She had been doing that all year at Bluford. But something had changed. Naveah felt it on her run, and though it made no sense, she couldn't stop herself. Her fingers blurred across the screen as she spelled out a reply.

Ten days. 9AM. School track, she wrote.

Would that be enough time for her to train and practice? She had no idea.

Before she could talk herself out of it, Naveah took a deep breath and posted her comment.

The responses came minutes later.

10 days! What u need 10 days for?

She ain't ready, that's why.

The comments kept coming the next morning. By then, Naveah discovered she had also gained a bunch of new followers, but she didn't care. Her mind focused on one comment that stood out among all the others.

See you there, JoniQuEEN11 had replied. You gonna get your butt handed to you.

"Ain't no way that's happening," Naveah said to herself, gripping her phone. "Ain't no way."

Chapter 5

"What'd I tell you?" Mom asked at dinner the night of her first radiation treatment. She had left her job at Little Learning Spot daycare early for her appointment, and she came home at her usual time as if nothing happened.

"I don't care what they say. I'm gonna work right through this thing," she declared, putting her hands on her hips proudly. Her voice was strong and slightly louder than usual as she gave Naveah and Christian hugs at the dinner table.

Naveah noticed Mom hadn't eaten much, and she fell asleep early on the couch, but otherwise she seemed completely fine. Naveah went to bed feeling hopeful, but that changed two days later when Mom had her first round of chemotherapy. Naveah had just returned from a long run through the busy neighborhood when her parents skidded to a stop outside their townhouse.

"Naveah! Give me a hand," Dad yelled, trying to help Mom out of the car. Naveah pocketed her phone and rushed to help. Her mother seemed like a different person than the one Naveah saw leave the house that morning. Her skin seemed washed out and slightly greenish, and she wobbled when she walked just like the time she drank too much at a New Year's party years ago. Dad steadied her by the elbow and led her inside.

"Mom!" Christian cried and raced toward her, but Naveah held him back.

"It's okay, it's okay," Dad assured him, but his voice was tinged with worry. "We just need to get to the bathroom," he added, steering Mom down the hallway as quickly as he could. He tried to close the door but didn't make it as Mom sank to her knees and threw up loudly.

"What's wrong with her?" Christian whimpered.

"She's gonna be all right," Dad snapped. "She just has nausea from the drugs they gave her. The doctors said it's normal. It'll settle down," he added before shutting the door.

"I thought medicine was supposed to make you better," Christian muttered.

"It is. But sometimes, things get worse before they get better," Naveah explained, slipping her arm around his shoulder. "Come on. Let's play Mario Kart," she offered, trying to distract him.

Mom went to bed early that night, and Dad stayed by her side. Naveah made canned soup and grilled cheese for dinner for her and Christian. In the heavy quiet after everyone had gone to bed, Naveah lay sleepless, her phone in hand, swiping robotically through cancer survival stories, track videos, and funny animal clips, when Jonique posted a new video.

This one showed her sprinting around Bluford's track at top speed…and then the camera cut to her feet, her sneakers charging out in front of her as first one foot and then the other sped across its red surface. When she slowed and stopped, the camera cut to her face.

"That's how a real one gets it done. Ain't no camera effect, you know what I'm sayin'?" She threw her hands up like a taunt.

Almost instantly, the post started getting "likes" and thumbs ups. Then comments began to appear.

That ain't no filter.
More than just 👟 ⚡⚡⚡

Oh no, Naveah thought. *Oh no, no*....

It was bad enough that Jonique had disrespected her in school, but now she was taking it where everyone could see it 24-7. Naveah pictured her new followers seeing it too.

Maybe she would lose them to Jonique as well?

She read Jonique's post again. She had to respond. But how?

Naveah imagined herself out on the track. She could put her phone on her selfie stick—or maybe prop it up somewhere so she could record herself running. Or maybe just film her feet, like Jonique's latest post.

But that would be weak, and people would say she was copying. That was the last thing she wanted. She needed something fresh. Something original. Something—

Her eyes tired and blurry, Naveah scrolled through social media searching for inspiration. She tried #running and that led to #girlswhorun, which led to #girlsontherun but still nothing clicked. As the moon outside began to set, Naveah swiped through an endless sea of images, videos, and how-to posts from influencer athletes until her mind grew foggy and her head drooped and...

She was on the track again, Jonique was right in front of her, almost side by side. But instead of gaining, Naveah was losing ground.

Jonique was pulling away from her. The crowd seemed to cheer, and then Naveah saw something else on the track with her. A figure. Dark and foreboding. Its feet pounded with each step. It was gaining on her. Closing distance. She turned to see a face sickly and diseased. It was stalking her with each pounding step. It reached out a withered hand, and tugged at her arm, trying to take her down.

No!

Naveah wrenched free and opened her eyes. Dad was at her side.

"Are you awake?" he said. "I kept knocking on your door, but you were zonked out."

"I'm up," she said, rubbing the spot on her arm where she had been grabbed in her dream.

"Good. Your mom is sleeping in. I gotta go to work. I'm trying to get extra hours this week to make up for lost time for all the treatments coming up. Can you check on her every hour or so? She was planning to work today but that's not happening," he sighed. "Doc said she might not be feeling good for a few days. And then there's another treatment

Thursday, so...we just gotta be patient and see how all this plays out."

Naveah remembered her dream and the awful sentence that had been haunting her since the day she read it.

Most pancreatic cancer patients live less than a year.

Naveah tried to shake the grim words out of her head, careful not to say anything to Dad.

He eyed her for a few long seconds before patting her on the shoulder.

"I gotta go. You'll look after them both, right?" He swallowed hard, then continued. "It's gonna be hard, Naveah. I'm not gonna lie. We gotta keep her spirits up. Maybe when she's feeling better, you can cheer her up a bit? Okay?"

How? How am I supposed to do that? Naveah wanted to say, but instead she nodded.

Dad kissed her forehead and left.

Mom stayed in bed until the early afternoon. Naveah checked on her constantly, pausing at the edge of the bedroom every half hour just to listen to her breathing. The last time Naveah checked, Mom had finally started to stir.

"Can you get me some water and some toast?" she asked, her voice scratchy and hoarse from sleep. Naveah was happy Mom asked for food, but when she placed the plate in front of her, Mom turned her head away.

"I can't yet," she muttered, waving her hand as if the toast somehow offended her. Puffy dark circles hung under her eyes, and her skin seemed to have thinned somehow, but Naveah was happy to see her sipping water at least.

Keep up her spirits, that's what Dad had suggested. Naveah tried to think of something happy to say, something that would bring a smile to her mother's weary face. But she couldn't think of a single thing, except—

"Mom, how do I get to be a fast runner? Fast enough to..." Naveah paused. She didn't want to tell her mother about Jonique's challenge or bring up the social media drama. That might make Mom take her phone away. "...maybe try out for the Bluford track team?" she finished in a hot rush of words.

Mom's brow wrinkled as if Naveah had asked if she could race to the moon with only a pair of sneakers. But then her eyes widened, and a smile lit up her face.

"That all depends," she said, sitting up and motioning for Naveah to join her on the bed. "How hard are you willing to work?"

Naveah thought about Jonique's taunts. "I'm serious, Mom."

Mom grabbed Naveah's hand and beamed. "Okay. Then you need to train. Just about every day. My secret was Baldwin Hill. Remember we used to go there when Christian was little?"

Naveah recalled the steep dusty hill that rose up and cut through the city several miles away. When Christian was still a toddler, Mom would sometimes take them there, and she would jog with him in a stroller, pushing him up the dusty trails that snaked through the sunbaked high ground. Naveah remembered the visitor center where they used to get ice cream when Mom finished her workouts. It seemed like a lifetime ago.

"When I was in high school, Coach Smalley had us run the trail up that hill twice each week. It was more cross country than track, but it gave us an edge. Where other schools were training on flat ground, we got stronger running uphill. I probably ran five hundred miles up and down Baldwin Hill back in the day," Mom explained, smiling at memories Naveah could not see.

"I remember that feeling when we were running back down, going so fast. It was like we were flying. Wish I could do that now. Maybe you can fly for me." Mom added, taking a sip of water and leaning back into her mattress. "I'm sorry, but that treatment really wore me out. I think I'm gonna lie down again, honey."

Naveah helped arrange Mom's pillows and pull the blanket around her. Then she kissed her mother's cheek and left the bedroom.

That night, unable to sleep, Naveah figured out how to respond to Jonique's post. The many "hearts" and comments told her that people were following the challenge. She knew some were waiting for her to respond.

Baldwin Hill would be her answer.

When morning came, Naveah found a pair of loose shorts and a tank top that would be good for a morning run. She tied her shoelaces tightly and headed for the kitchen.

Dad was already at the table with his head propped on his hands and his phone pressed against his ear.

"You don't understand." Dad spoke in a low and calm voice, but Naveah noticed his foot shaking the way it did whenever he got stressed. "She might not be...well enough to come back to the daycare for a while."

The caller must have said something positive because he nodded and grunted a few times. "Thank you, Stephanie," he said finally. "And please thank Tarah for being willing to work Amaya's shifts this summer," he added before hanging up, seeming both exhausted and relieved. Naveah noticed he was surrounded by stacks of papers, a Patient's Rights booklet from the hospital, and a bag containing several brown pill bottles, which he pushed aside when their eyes met.

"Why are you up so early?"

"I'm going to run up Baldwin Hill before it gets hot," Naveah said, grabbing a bottle of water from the refrigerator.

"Baldwin Hill?"

"Yeah. Mom said she used to run there to train," Naveah said. "I'm training now, so I want to check it out. How's Mom doing?"

Dad glanced at the stack of papers and the pill bottles and shrugged his shoulders. For a second, he almost seemed lost.

"She was better without the chemo, that's for sure," he admitted finally, taking a deep breath. "Your mom chose to be aggressive with her cancer treatments, and the doctors agreed, so this is what we get. She's gonna feel pretty lousy for a while."

Dad's phone began to vibrate with an incoming call. He glanced at it quickly.

"It's one of Mom's docs. I gotta take this," he blurted. Naveah waved and left.

The noisy bus ride to Baldwin Hill Park took twenty minutes. But when Naveah stepped off the bus, she felt as if she had wandered onto a whole new planet. The grid of highways with low slung shopping plazas, fast food restaurants, and dollar stores had given way to a rocky cluster of low hills that rose above the city. Like something Christian might build in Minecraft, the high ground was bordered by an area of shrubs, scraggly trees and rocks that obscured the view of the surrounding neighborhoods. Pathways and trails snaked upward at different points toward the summit.

Naveah stared up at the peak. It was craggy and steep, and she was surprised to feel excitement thrumming in her chest at the thought of telling Mom about how she had conquered it. Maybe it would make her smile and feel a little better, Naveah hoped.

Naveah fished her phone out of her pocket. Her reply to Jonique's post required her phone's camera and stopwatch. She quickly recorded the path entrance then pointed the camera so the summit was visible. She would aim the phone at her feet as she ran up the hill. At the top, she'd switch to the stopwatch and record her time. Maybe she would say something too with the city in the distance behind her. Would that be "real" enough?

It better be, she figured, hitting "record" on her phone.

"Okay," she said aloud, dropping her usual Klassy Kay voice and speaking naturally. "Baldwin Hill's about to go down." Then she started the timer and launched up the trail, holding her phone in her palm to record her feet.

For the first few yards, the trail was packed hard, and it was easy to run fast. But as the path climbed, the ground became soft and unsteady beneath her feet, sapping her power and making her run harder. The sun blasted down on her arms and face, and sweat made her tank top cling to her back. Naveah leaned into the incline, feeling the strain in her quads and hamstrings without slowing her pace. It felt good to be moving again, letting her body—not her mind—take control. Naveah surrendered to it and let her legs lead the way.

The path curved into a switchback and then ascended again. Naveah powered forward and upward, the toes of her shoes landing *one-two one-two* in the brown earth. Her legs were still willing, so she maintained her pace, though her heart was hammering, and she could hear the whooshing of her breath with each step.

Naveah had seen no one on the path as she raced upwards. But suddenly, as she rounded the switchback, a man appeared ahead of her. Unwilling to stop or lose time, Naveah shifted to one side and darted past the hunched figure toiling slowly up the steep hill. A charcoal hoodie hid his face.

"Hey!" he cried and stumbled as Naveah raced by.

"Sorry," Naveah yelled, pushing herself harder.

The summit was in sight. Naveah lifted her head and squinted against the sweat that stung her eyes and blurred her vision. Her muscles were beginning to ache, and her breath could not come quick enough, but still she forced herself up the hill as fast as she could. Maybe as fast as Mom had run it all those years ago.

And then, right when she thought her heart might explode with the effort of the climb, the ground leveled beneath her feet.

She flipped her phone up, stopping the timer and the camera. She slowed to a walk and shook out her legs which burned from exertion. Sweat dripped down her face, but Naveah ignored it, closing her eyes and bringing her breath back under control. Finally, she glanced at the time. 10:48.

Naveah imagined her mother, years younger, standing in the same spot.

"Hey!" someone shouted, shattering her thought. The man she had passed on the trail suddenly came huffing up the summit. "You almost knocked me over!"

Naveah jumped, ready to call 9-1-1 or bolt back down the hill if he were to come closer. But then, the man pulled down his hood, and Kareem Burnett stood in front of her. Sweat trickled down his forehead and a huge smile stretched across his face.

"Kareem! Sorry! I didn't recognize you!"

"That's 'cause you were running too fast," he laughed, resting his hands on his hips in exhaustion. "You ran up that hill like a mountain lion. For a second, I thought you were gonna knock me over, and I'd roll all the way back down." He slipped a small backpack off his shoulder and pulled out two water bottles. He handed one to her and took a gulp from the other.

"I'm really sorry. I was just so focused on training," she explained, thanking him for the water. She was unsure whether to mention Jonique or that she had recorded the run.

"It's all good. I'm glad to see you out here training. I can't wait to watch your rematch."

He pulled out his phone and his fingers flashed across the screen. In a second, Naveah caught a quick glance of the video of her racing Jonique on the school track.

"You need to beat her. I can't stand that girl!" He paused to gulp more water.

Naveah smiled at his comment and took a quick drink. She wondered how many other people at Bluford felt the same way.

"What are you even doing out here?" she asked. "This is like the middle of nowhere."

Kareem grinned. "Nah, this hill's my secret. Actually, it's where the cross country team practices sometimes. I've been coming here for months to train for football. If I make wide receiver, running here will be one reason why. You'd be surprised what carrying some water bottles up this hill ten times will do to you."

Naveah nodded and smiled. She had noticed he had become more chiseled and cut during the school year. She could see it now as she glanced at his chest and felt herself blush awkwardly. He pointed to the phone still in her hand.

"Hey, were you recording a video? Wait. Were you about to clap back at Jonique?"

"Maybe," she replied coyly.

"For real!? Oooh!!!" he cheered, leaning in closer to her phone. "Lemme see?"

Naveah hesitated. *What if it's stupid*, she thought. "I'm not sure—"

"C'mon, Naveah! Somebody needs to answer that girl's nonsense," Kareem insisted. "That girl needs a lesson. You look like the person who could teach her."

"I didn't make a lesson," Naveah explained. "I just recorded my run."

"Let me see."

Reluctantly Naveah unlocked her phone. The rocky brown landscape of Baldwin Hill filled the small screen and began to zoom past. Then Naveah's feet appeared. They zipped over the ground, leaping over rocks and devouring the steep trail in long strides. Naveah's breathing and the whoosh of the air moving past was the only sound—until she nearly collided with Kareem before dashing past. His muffled voice shouted "Hey!" in the distance.

"Whoa!" Kareem said, glancing at her in awe. "I knew you were fast, but this clip is fire. You crushed that hill, and you make it look easy!"

"You think so? They'll probably think I sped it up or faked it or—"

"What if I prove you didn't? I can be your witness," he suggested, his eyes sincere and warm. "Can I see your phone?" he asked, holding his hand out.

She handed it to him and watched as Kareem stretched out his long arm so that Naveah and the distant skyline were included in the frame. Then he hit record.

"Y'all, it's KareemdaDream. And let me tell you, Naveah just killed that hill!" He shook a finger at the camera. "All I gotta say is some people need to look out! She's gonna give 'em a run for that money! Peace!"

He stopped the recording and handed her phone back. "How's that?"

Naveah smiled and shrugged, unsure whether to hit post.

"I know one person who's not gonna like it," she admitted, picturing Jonique's face.

"True," he said, zipping up his backpack and gazing at the city below them. "But what will really upset her is if you win. I'd pay to see that."

"*If* I win?"

He smiled. "*When* you win, I mean."

"That's better." She smiled shyly.

"You know I'm gonna be there rooting for you," he added. "Wouldn't miss it."

Naveah's smile widened. Sparks of excitement danced invisibly in the air.

"Race you back down?" she asked, taking off before he could reply.

Chapter 6

Naveah was happy to find Mom sitting on the couch when she returned from Baldwin Hill. Yet her color seemed off somehow, as though she had been lit with a bad filter that made her look almost yellowish. Fine lines seemed to have appeared overnight around her eyes and mouth too. Mom's hand rested on her stomach protectively, as if she was trying to soothe it from the outside. Plastic pill bottles, a glass of water, and an old pot cluttered the table next to her.

All Naveah's excitement about the video with Kareem evaporated instantly.

"Hey, baby," Mom said. Naveah could tell she was trying hard to sound like her usual self. "So, you did it? Went up Baldwin Hill?" She struggled to sit up. "How was it?"

"Good." She showed her mother a clip of the video she had made on her phone, careful not to include Kareem's part. "See?"

"You filmed it!?" Mom exclaimed. "All you kids need a break from your phones, especially when you're running." Her mother huffed. But her eyes sparked when the video began to play. "Oh my God, look at that hill. It's exactly the same! Look at you go!" she exclaimed. "How long it take you to go up and back?"

Naveah shook her head. "I didn't time the down run." She didn't want to mention running into Kareem and getting distracted. Mom might make a big deal out of it, and Naveah wasn't sure what "it" was. Still, Naveah couldn't forget the flutter in her stomach when he had stood near her.

"Keep time from now on. How else will you know if you're improving? Back in the day, I could do it in 17 minutes 21 seconds. That's 5K." Mom said proudly. "I ever tell you that?"

All the time, Naveah thought. But she shook her head and said, "No."

"You wouldn't believe it to look at me now," Mom chuckled. "I was the fastest girl on the team. Skinny as a rail, just like you! Not anymore," she said, shaking her head slowly.

Naveah wasn't sure what to say. Yes, Mom's hips and belly were nothing like the athlete pictured in Bluford's trophy case, but they were good and natural and always part of the Mom she knew. Yet now they seemed a bit smaller. What had also changed recently, Naveah noticed again, was the yellowish tone in her mother's skin and the dark circles under her eyes.

"Well, I know I ain't looking or feeling great today," Mom explained, seeming to sense Naveah's thoughts. "To be honest, I didn't expect my treatment to be so rough. But these new medicines should make the next ones easier," she said, pointing to the pill bottles on the table.

"So...the doctors think it's working?" Naveah asked.

Mom sighed and returned her hand to her stomach as if a fresh stab of pain hit her.

"Too early to tell for sure, but I'll say this much. It better be working if it's gonna make me this sick! I can't do anything stuck on the couch like this."

"Maybe you can help me," Naveah suggested, eager to offer something—anything—to help her mother focus on something positive. And yet, Naveah realized, she needed it too.

"Anything, baby. What do you need?"

"So, Mom, I got up the hill fast, but I was so out of breath it felt like I was going to..."

Die. Naveah caught the word in her throat. It wasn't something she wanted to say to her mother—not even in a joke—yet Mom smiled back at her.

"Die?" Mom declared. "Oh, I been there. Feels like you're going to throw up too!" Mom nodded at the pot on the table. "That happens when you're pushing your hardest. But if you build up your strength and endurance, you can go longer without feeling that way. You shouldn't feel like you're dying when you run. Instead, you wanna feel strong and powerful. It may seem strange, but running was my happy place when I was your age. It's where I found myself growing up."

Naveah remembered how she felt churning up Baldwin Hill, her legs powering her forward, her thoughts roaming free. She recalled the satisfaction of chasing down Jonique on the track too, watching the distance between them melt away. In that moment, everything else had disappeared. Naveah had escaped feeling worried about school, or what anyone thought or said about her, or what might happen in the future.

"It was like freedom for me," Mom admitted.

"Same."

Naveah suddenly felt close to her mother, as if a great divide had been crossed, at least for a moment. Her mother seemed to feel it too.

"I didn't know you were so into running, Naveah," Mom said finally. "I always knew you'd be good at it, but the only thing you seemed to care about this year was your phone. What's changed?"

Naveah thought about telling her about Jonique and the upcoming race, but then held back. Mom looked better. She was sitting up straight. Some of the sparkle in her eyes had returned. Naveah didn't want to ruin it.

"I just want to get faster," she said. "Like, right away."

"Then we need to make you a training program!" Mom beamed. "I can help." She swung her legs off the couch and gestured for Naveah to move closer.

Naveah scooted next to her, inhaling the familiar scent of Mom's lavender body wash. But there was another smell lurking beneath it: medications and a sour new chemical odor.

Hiding her reaction, Naveah grabbed her phone and took notes as Mom hammered out a plan.

Naveah dropped her backpack on the shiny silver ledge of the Bluford bleachers and pulled out her water bottle a week later. It was barely 9:00 a.m., and the air was already warm and sticky. *Another tough running day*, Naveah thought. She took a sip of water and headed onto the track.

"Heat training can be a huge speed advantage," Mom had said the other day, but Naveah had her doubts. Her mother made her watch a YouTube video featuring a Kenyan runner whose lean, pencil-thin body and muscled legs spoke of years of training. She mentioned how running miles in 100-degree heat had helped her win an Olympic medal. The whole time she was talking, though, Naveah had been thinking of Kareem.

Two days ago, she had decided to post the video she'd filmed with him. Already it had more "likes" and comments than anything she had ever posted. She wondered if Kareem was serious when he said he would be there for her race with Jonique.

She hoped so.

One week to go. Naveah pushed the thought out of her mind and focused on her mother's instructions for this morning's run.

"Run as fast as you can for one lap, then do a slow jog for the next the one. Repeat this five times. Understand?" Mom had said.

She was going with Dad to the hospital for radiation treatment. Her voice had sounded strong, but her color still hadn't returned. Naveah knew Mom hadn't been eating much either. Her nausea was almost constant, and lately Mom's clothes seemed looser. This morning, Naveah spotted an area on Mom's scalp where her hair had thinned. Everything matched what Naveah had read about cancer treatments.

"Next week, you'll do two laps before slowing down, then three, then four," Mom had explained just before Naveah left. "This will build your endurance, and in time you'll get faster," Mom finished.

Time. It was the one thing Naveah didn't have.

Naveah stared at the empty track and felt a twinge of nerves. What if the race in gym class had been luck and nothing more? What if Jonique really had slowed down and let her catch up? What if Jonique beat her? It would be on everyone's phones within seconds, and there would be no way to escape or outrun it at Bluford High. The thought made her stomach churn.

Naveah knew she needed to start running before it got any hotter, but instead she grabbed her phone, careful to avoid Instagram where she might see more comments about the race. Instead, out of habit, she took a quick selfie to show confidence. But when she looked at the pic, a scared, skinny-faced girl stared back at her.

Naveah deleted the pic and arranged another photo, this time of her lead foot against the white starting line. She snapped and posted it quickly before opening her stopwatch app. Sweat was already beading on her back when she skipped a few feet along the track's red surface to warm up. Her legs felt loose and springy as she counted down to her start.

Three, two, one...

With a deep breath, Naveah shot forward, sprinting the loop of the track as fast as she could. She had planned to slow down for the second lap as Mom had suggested, but Jonique's posted mile time from the All-City competition taunted her.

5:47.

Naveah decided to skip the plan and keep running. The race with Jonique would be four laps. Why not run her best now and see how her time compared to Jonique's? She figured Mom would say the same thing if she knew about the upcoming race. Pressing on to the second lap, Naveah fought the urge to glance at her stopwatch.

Eyes forward. Never look back. Mom had told her, and she listened.

A burning feeling began to creep into her legs and scald her lungs. Sweat stung her eyes and blurred her vision. Her lungs started craving more air, more oxygen, more fuel. The pace, so much faster than at Baldwin Hill, hurt. Part of her wanted to stop, to rest, to make the ache go away. But Naveah thought of Mom and willed herself through lap three.

Her breath shallow and quick as she rounded the final lap, Naveah broke into a wild, all-out sprint for the last hundred yards. As she crossed the finish line, she hit the stop button on the app, her chest heaving, her stomach cramping. She jogged a bit further, then slowed to a walk and waited for her breathing and heart rate to recover.

Fifty yards later, Naveah finally stepped off the track onto the grass. It was time to look. She lifted the phone to her face, telling herself she would be happy with anything under six minutes.

There, etched in glowing numbers on the phone's face, was her time:

5:54.

Excitement flooded Naveah's weary body. She stared at the number to make sure it was real. Then she took a quick screenshot.

She was about to send the pic to Kareem and post it when she heard laughter from the far side of the track. Naveah looked up to see Malika and Jonique approaching the starting area. They were talking but stopped suddenly when they made eye contact with her. Naveah was sure they had been talking about her. She quickly moved toward the bleachers to grab her stuff and leave.

"Hey!" Malika called out. "Hey, Naveah! Wait! Stop!"

Naveah looked for a way to avoid them, but the only other exit was through the high school, and the building was locked for the summer. With a sigh, she slowed and turned toward the girls.

"What you doin' here?" Jonique demanded. She wore Bluford High track shorts and a white running tank. Her muscles seemed to shimmer in the afternoon sun. She eyed Naveah impatiently, as if she were looking at an unwanted guest.

"Running," Naveah responded.

"You ready for the race?" Malika asked. She wore black running shorts and a yellow Bluford Track T-shirt. Her braids were pinned up off her shoulders and held back by a headband. She sounded eager and excited.

Naveah shrugged.

"She scared is what she is," Jonique said smugly. "She knows she gonna get beat—"

Naveah thrust her phone under the girl's nose. "*You* should be scared. See that? That's my mile time. That's what I just did."

Malika's eyes widened at the numbers. Jonique glanced at them and smirked. "Girl, get outta my face. Anybody can run a stopwatch and stop it on any number they want—"

"Yeah, but that's not me. I just ran that time!"

"So? I got you beat. Besides, nothing counts except next Wednesday. None of the stuff you postin' counts." Jonique folded her arms over her chest. "Come on, Malika. We got work to do."

Jonique turned away but Malika studied Naveah for a long moment. When she followed Jonique back onto the track, she said something in a low voice that Naveah heard clearly.

"We could use her on the team."

"No. No way—"

"But she's *fast*, J! We need her. We'll win All City for sure if we get one more distance runner."

"Naw, she won't last more than a lap or two—"

"Coach Sherman can help her with that," Malika's voice was soft and persuasive. "You know how good she is with conditioning—"

"Forget it, Malika. Wait till next week. You'll see."

Then they started running and their voices dropped away.

Naveah watched them jog around the track. They moved together with confidence and strength as teammates and friends. Next to them, Naveah knew she was an outsider. The loneliness she had felt her entire first year at Bluford swept over her.

Naveah turned away and glanced down at her phone as if it offered an escape. The stopwatch app still showed 5:54 on the small black screen. She also noticed the picture she had posted of her foot on the starting line had dozens of "likes" and comments. She even had a few more followers on Instagram. One comment from KareemdaDream345 stood out.

Go get it, Lightning Legs.

Naveah smiled and closed the app. One way or the other, the clash with Jonique would come soon enough. "Wednesday, 9:00 a.m.," Naveah said to herself. She could barely wait.

Chapter 7

"I'm gonna need your help tomorrow, Naveah," Dad said at dinner the night before the race.

"Okay," Naveah agreed, her eyes locked on her phone. She was scrolling through last-minute racing tips on "Black Girls Run," a blog Mom shared with her as part of her training program.

"This'll be more useful than that Klassy Kay, or whatever her name is," Mom proclaimed when she shared it. So far, she had been right. Naveah reread the post for the third time, repeating each tip to herself so she wouldn't forget.

Get good sleep.
Eat a high-carb meal.
Drink plenty of water.

Naveah took another gulp of water and placed a large forkful of spaghetti into her mouth. Her legs twitched with excitement as she imagined herself flying around the track. Could she beat Jonique? The thought of so many people watching made her stomach tremble.

"Naveah? Did you hear me?" Dad snapped. "Can you put the phone down, please?"

"Okay," she grumbled, laying her phone down and trying to hide her annoyance. After all, Christian had on his headphones and was staring at his tablet like always. Yet Dad never said anything to him. Mom would never have let them eat at the table with their devices, but she was in the bedroom resting, as usual. She hadn't eaten at the dinner table in days.

"Mom's next chemo is tomorrow morning," Dad began, rubbing his temples slowly like he had a bad headache. He looked as if he had not slept in days. "I been shifting my schedule every which way to be here and be with Mom. But there's no one to cover my route early tomorrow." He shook his head wearily.

"So maybe just reschedule," Naveah suggested. Dad shook his head.

"These treatments are her best shot, Naveah," he explained. "She needs them on a regular schedule for them to be effective.

We don't want her to miss or change any of that. You understand?"

Naveah nodded, wondering what her father wanted her to do.

"I can take Christian to Little Learning Spot for the day. Mrs. Stephanie and Tarah Carson will watch him for us. I'll drop you guys off at the hospital by 8:30. I know Mom's not gonna want to take the bus afterwards, so you'll need to get a cab or Uber to bring her home—"

"Wait," Naveah interrupted, her head beginning to spin. "You want me to go to her treatment?" The idea of watching her mother undergo a medical procedure was terrifying. And then there was the race. Naveah realized what Dad was asking would make her miss it. "But I can't—"

"I need you, Naveah. Mom needs you."

"But tomorrow—"

"Look, all you'll have to do is sit in the waiting room for an hour or so and then…" he sighed wearily. "Then you help get her home. If I can get someone to cover for me, I'll be there. But just in case I can't," his voice dropped. "I need you to help out. You know how it goes after these treatments."

Naveah winced. She had seen Mom go through several treatments already, and each one seemed to leave her weaker than the last.

"But does it have to be tomorrow morning?"

Dad frowned. "Yes, Naveah. I told you. These doses are Mom's best shot to—"

"But can't we do it in the afternoon or the next day?" she pleaded, thinking of the race and all the hype on her posts. "Does it have to be tomorrow morning?"

"Why? What's up tomorrow?"

Naveah was about to tell Dad about the race at the track but then stopped herself. Compared to Mom's treatments, it sounded unimportant and silly. Naveah shook her head. "I was just gonna…never mind," she finished, then added quickly, "I can be there for her."

Can't race you tomorrow. Thursday instead?
Did that sound right?
Can't race in the morning. Can we race later in the day?
Was that better?
Looking forward to beating you but need to do it at a different time. You pick.
Too challenging. Too confident.

Naveah typed and erased the message over and over again. What to say? Should she send a direct message to Jonique? Or should she post her message to her account and tag Jonique so everyone could see it? Kareem and a few other Bluford students had said they were coming to watch, but Naveah wondered if that was even true.

Do I have to say anything at all? Naveah wondered. For a moment, she imagined what could happen if people showed up at the track and she wasn't there.

"Told you she was scared," Jonique would say with her hand on her hips and satisfaction on her face. *"I knew she wouldn't show. She knew she'd get beat."*

Naveah's stomach flipped just imagining Jonique's smug face. She bent over her phone and started again.

Jonique, can we race another day? My mom is sick, and I have to go with her to the hospital.

Naveah stared at the words. They were simple and true. And it seemed fair to reach out to Jonique directly instead of posting something for everyone.

She hit "send" and waited. If Jonique were online, she might answer right away. But when five minutes became thirty and then stretched into an hour, and still no response came, Naveah began to wonder if she had made a mistake.

"Naveah! You ready?" Dad boomed, knocking hard on her bedroom door. "We gotta go!"

Naveah sat up, surprised to see the morning sun streaming through her window. Her phone was still on the bed next to her, where she kept it waiting to hear from Jonique. She grabbed it to look for updates, but the screen stayed dark. She realized she had never plugged it in.

"C'mon, Naveah!" Dad opened the door just as she climbed out of bed. "Get off that phone and get dressed. There's no time this morning," he yelled.

"I'm coming," she snapped, reaching for a clean T-shirt and her shoes. "Two minutes."

Dad muttered angrily under his breath and slammed the door so she could get dressed.

They arrived tense and quiet at the hospital a short time later.

"Have a seat. They'll call you when they're ready," grumbled the male nurse at the reception desk when Mom checked in. He pointed to rigid chairs arranged in clusters throughout the waiting area. Mom nodded and headed toward an empty seat in the nearest corner. Seeing her out in public under the harsh fluorescent light of the hospital, Naveah was struck by how much her mother had changed.

Only a month ago, most of her clothes were snug over her shoulders. Now her blouse looked baggy and oversized. Mom was walking differently too. Normally she would cross a room in long easy strides, but today she moved slowly, as if each step took effort. But what stood out most to Naveah was Mom's hair. Once thick and black, it had thinned noticeably, and small bald patches of her scalp were visible.

Naveah pretended not to see as she sat down next to Mom and spotted the clock on the wall. It was almost 9:00.

The race.

"Is there somewhere I can charge my phone?" Naveah asked a passing nurse's aide in navy blue scrubs and thick glasses.

"The main lobby by the elevators or the cafeteria," the aide grumbled, seeming bothered by the question, but Naveah couldn't help it. She wondered if Jonique had answered her message or rescheduled their race. Naveah wanted to run to the lobby to charge, but she knew she couldn't leave Mom alone. Frustrated, she shoved the dead phone in her pocket and waited.

That's when she noticed the other people seated in the waiting area. A young hollow-eyed woman, her head wrapped in a maroon scarf, sat alone across from them. A middle-aged man with a cane and a head bandage slouched in a chair behind her. He held hands with a nervous-looking blonde woman who hovered close, studying his face intently. A slender elderly lady nodded off in the back corner of the room. A younger man—her son, Naveah figured—hunched in the seat next to her, filling out forms.

All of them were likely battling cancer too, Naveah realized. It was a secret war that she had never witnessed, a fight that made her frustration about her phone seem small and petty.

Just then, the heavy doors outside the treatment area opened and a new nurse stepped into the waiting room, an electronic tablet in her hand. "Amaya Kendrick?" she called.

Naveah helped her mother to the doorway. As soon as the nurse ushered Mom inside, Naveah rushed to the lobby area to charge. Within minutes, her phone began to buzz with a flurry of notifications and messages.

Where u at?
Can't believe u didn't show!

You left me hanging!

And finally, the words: Check this, followed by a link.

Naveah clicked and saw a video of Jonique standing on Bluford's track in her racing singlet.

"So, I'm here, y'all, and ready to run. But guess who ain't?" She spun her camera around to show the desolate track. The camera lingered on the faces of the gathered "crowd"—just a few people, really—standing on the track or sitting in the bleachers. Naveah spotted Malika and Kareem right away, and she recognized other members of Bluford's track team before Jonique swung the camera back to her smug face.

"Some of y'all might be surprised. Not me. *Some* people like to talk tough, pretending they something when they ain't nothing. Then at the last minute, they got some sad excuse. You know that girl texted me 'my mama sick' last night? Yeah, right. You ought to be ashamed of a lie like that." Jonique shook her head. "We all know the real reason she didn't show."

"What?!" Naveah exclaimed in the crowded hospital lobby. Shock, anger and hurt washed over her in waves as the video continued.

Jonique handed her phone to someone else. Seconds later, she was sprinting away, legs and arms pumping furiously. No doubt, she was quick, maybe faster than ever, Naveah noticed.

"That's why!" Jonique beamed into the camera triumphantly after her short sprint. "I'm a real one. This here's *my* track. Don't nobody forget it."

The video ended, but Naveah kept staring, her mind storming at Jonique's words.

I reached out to you!
I told you the truth!
All I asked for was time!

Naveah wanted to shout for the whole world to hear, yet already comments were appearing under Jonique's video.

She a coward.
Bad karma to lie like that.
Hope her mom really does get sick.
She messed around. Now she gonna find out.

Naveah cursed and nearly threw her phone in disgust. She yanked her charge cable from the wall and stormed back to the waiting room, her pulse pounding harder than her final sprint up Baldwin Hill.

"I'll prove it," she told herself.

Grabbing a seat by the nursing station, Naveah lifted her phone and snapped a selfie in the waiting area. She posted it immediately, hoping the image would show everyone the truth. But within seconds negative responses filled her screen.

You ought to be ashamed, lyin' like that.
This girl has serious problems.
Stop with the fake pics!
Might be true, though.

The last one was posted by a familiar account. KareemdaDream345. Naveah frowned. *Might* be true? *Might?*

He had defended her in English class and on Baldwin Hill, but now he didn't seem sure.

Naveah looked around the waiting area angrily. Maybe she could take another picture? A picture with the date or another person?

She stood up and turned so that she could frame herself and the nursing station in her phone's camera. That's when she noticed the young woman with the head scarf watching her. Her unblinking brown eyes and pained face stunned Naveah. She looked at her own face in the phone screen and hated what she was doing. It seemed so wrong to intrude on the poor woman and her fellow patients. She knew Mom would be furious with her too.

"Miss, put that camera away," boomed a voice from behind her. Naveah turned to face the stern-faced aide from earlier. He pointed angrily at her phone. "This is a hospital, and patients have a right to privacy. Filming is not permitted here. Turn it off, or I'll call security."

Naveah could feel many eyes in the room staring at her in disapproval, and she agreed with them. Yet she hated that people were lying about her and that complete strangers were joining in. Their posts were mean, wrong, untrue, and yet they kept coming. Notifications buzzed her phone like mad rabid bees.

"I'm sorry," Naveah replied, her face searing with embarrassment and shame.

Naveah's phone continued to flash with notifications and comments when Mom emerged from her treatment woozy and weak and trying not to retch. On the slow Uber ride home, Naveah put the phone down to hold Mom's hands as she struggled to not get sick in the car. It was then Naveah decided, for the first time ever, that she was done with social media.

"You haven't been running as much," Mom said, taking a weak sip of tea.

Two weeks had passed since she missed the race against Jonique. That night Naveah deleted every one of her social media apps. She knew it did not solve her issues with

Jonique, but it was better than seeing her nonsense day and night all summer.

"No," Naveah admitted. She hadn't told her mother what happened at the hospital, and she wasn't about to, especially not after watching Mom's daily struggles. She had continued to lose weight and now wore scarves to hide her thinning hair. Simple tasks like standing up were getting harder—so much harder that Dad had brought home a walker and a portable wheelchair for her. So far, Mom refused to use them.

"I can get around just fine," she had declared the night he brought them home. The walker sat unused in the corner of the living room, while the wheelchair stayed folded up in the closet. On good days, Mom could get herself from her bed to the couch, though she often had to grip the wall or lean on someone to make it. Sometimes, the effort left her exhausted and she would fall asleep after reaching her destination. There were more pills, too. Some treated her cancer, and others were supposed to relieve the side effects of radiation and chemo. But despite all the medicines, Mom was still in pain, something Naveah could see her trying to hide, even now.

"So why aren't you running?"

"I just been busy," Naveah lied. She set a protein drink on the folding tray next to her mother's chair. "Please drink it, Mom. You know what the doctor said about getting more nutrition."

Mom ignored the drink and stared at Naveah. "You know cross country tryouts are in a few weeks. They still do them at Baldwin Hill. I keep thinking you should go out for it." A tired smile lit her thinning face. "You know, family legacy and all that. Those long skinny legs give you an advantage in distance races. Trust me, I know. And the way you raced up that hill in that video?!" Mom shook her head. "Bluford's got a good team. You'd make 'em better!"

Naveah could not shake the ugly words people said about her in their posts. She knew some came from possible teammates at Bluford. All the drama would start again, and it would be even worse. A fresh wave of anger blazed inside her.

"I'm not interested."

"What?" Mom blinked in confusion. "Why not?"

Naveah shrugged and crossed her arms. "I probably wouldn't make it. Like you said, they already got a good team." She tried to sound as if she didn't care. "Besides, they don't want me."

Mom put her tea down with a thud. Naveah felt her mother's gaze focus on her like a spotlight. She wondered if her mom knew what really happened with Jonique. Back in middle school, Mom used to monitor her social media from time to time to see what she posted. It was long ago, but maybe she had been doing it again now that she was stuck at home.

"Naveah, I know I've been struggling," Mom began, taking a deep breath. "I can't do most of what I used to do, and not even half of what I *need* to do. We've asked so much from you—from shopping and cooking and looking after Chris. I know I'll need your help until…" her voice faltered. "Until I get better. But I don't want you to stop running to take care of me—"

"No, Mom! That's not it!" Naveah sat down next to her and grabbed her hand. It was slender and delicate, but also soft and warm. "It's just…"

Naveah searched for an answer her mother would accept.

"There are some girls on the team who don't like me very much," she confessed. "We got into it over…a project at school at the end of the year," she added quickly before her mother could ask questions. "No big deal. Just..." Naveah shrugged. "You know. School."

Mom frowned. "A project?" She asked knowingly. "Or was it a race?"

Naveah felt something collapse inside her. An invisible wall crashed down. Mom reached out and stroked Naveah's face with her soft, thin hand and smiled sadly.

"I'm sorry you missed your race because of me."

Tears welled in Naveah's eyes.

"I don't care about that—"

"Of course, you do! And you should!" Mom interrupted angrily. "You woulda whooped that girl's behind, too!" she laughed, wiping away Naveah's tears. "And trust me, I remember them days. Girls can be so mean. But you can't let them stop you. Try out for the team, Naveah. If you make it, they'll shut up. They may not like you, but they'll respect you—"

"But what if I don't make it?" Naveah interrupted. "They could get worse—"

"You'll make it."

"But—"

"I know it's scary, Naveah, I do. But you don't wanna stay on the sidelines missing out on your life just because of some girl's dumb comments. Don't let that happen, you hear me?" Mom pleaded. The words stirred in Naveah's chest.

"That day you ran Baldwin Hill something special happened. I saw it. Even Chris mentioned it. Running gave you a goal and a purpose. It made you stronger. You gotta run with it....You see what I did there?" A smile flickered on Mom's face.

"To be honest, maybe that's what I need too. A goal," Mom continued. "Fighting this cancer…it's hard. Really hard." She inhaled deeply and sighed. "Sometimes, I wonder if…if I'm gonna win."

Naveah hugged her mother then, pressing herself into the loose fabric of Mom's shirt. "You got this, Mom," she murmured. "I know it!"

Mom squeezed Naveah back and then pulled away, wiping her eyes quickly. "Well, I'm going to keep fighting. That's for certain. And if I can do that, you can try out for cross country. Wouldn't it be somethin' if both of us got pictures in that trophy case?" Mom paused as if she was seeing the image in her mind. "So…are you in?"

Naveah stared into her mother's face. Hope and determination glimmered in Mom's eyes. They made her look stronger than she had in weeks. Naveah took a deep breath, knowing her answer was as much for her mother as it was for herself.

"Okay," she agreed. "I'll do it. I'll try out."

A grin spread across Mom's face. "That's it! You got this. Those girls won't have nothing to say when you make the team." Mom hesitated, then smiled again. "And I'm gonna get myself together so I can take you to tryouts. Yeah," she said, more to herself than to Naveah. "We'll go to Baldwin Hill together. You'll see. Now hand me that protein drink."

Naveah obeyed, and Mom took a swig from the bottle and grimaced. "I think you gonna have to help me get to the bathroom," she began, then stopped and gestured for the walker.

"Hand me that thing, Naveah," she said. "I gotta practice moving on my own."

Naveah rushed to place the walker in her grasp. Mom gripped the frame and slowly stepped forward, grunting with effort. She then shifted it forward and took two more steps before pausing to rest.

"You see, Naveah?" Mom smiled weakly. "I'm training, too."

Chapter 8

The late summer sun pounded the street as Naveah headed out to Bluford's track early the next morning. If she was going to try out for cross country and face all the rumors, doubts, and gossip, Naveah knew she had to get ready.

She hoped to complete a workout before anyone else arrived at the school. But as she ducked under the bulky padlock chains at Bluford's track entrance, she spotted a familiar figure in a hoodie trudging around by himself.

Kareem.

His head was down, and Naveah hoped he hadn't seen her. She quickly turned to leave, when she heard his voice call out.

"Naveah! Wait! Hold up."

A tremor of anger rippled through her as he trotted over. She recalled how he had responded to her news that Mom was in the hospital.

Might be true, he had said, as if she could lie about such a thing. The memory made Naveah want to rip Bluford's gate wide open, but Kareem smiled as if nothing had happened, as if there had never been a race she missed.

"What is it, Kareem?" Naveah grunted impatiently, fighting the urge to walk away.

The smile slid off his face. "Where have you been? I ain't talked to you in like forever—"

"You mean since the day of the race?" Naveah snapped. "You got something you wanna ask me since you don't know what *might be* true? Or are you just like everyone who called me a liar?"

Kareem frowned. "Hey, I'm nothing like those people. I know they ain't been nice—"

"Nice?" Naveah's shouted. "They're mean and messed up, and all they do is lie. What I said was true. My mom's got cancer. And that morning I was at the hospital with her. Did you actually think I'd lie about that?"

"No, I mean..." he stammered. "I just remembered your mom was like some super athlete or whatever, and you never mentioned her being sick before so...I wasn't sure."

"You weren't sure?!" Naveah almost spat the words. "So why didn't you ask me?"

"I've tried for weeks! You ghosted me ever since."

"What about that morning," Naveah fumed, ignoring him. "Instead of asking me, you posted how what I said '*might* be true.' *Might* be. Like I could lie about what my poor mom is going through!" She groaned. "I'm not surprised Jonique would say that, but you? I can't." Naveah's voice cracked and she turned away.

Kareem reached for her arm. "Aw, man," he breathed. "Naveah, I totally messed up, okay? I know you're better than that. The whole thing got crazy, and everyone was saying dumb stuff. You know how it is on social media sometimes," he said, shaking his head. "I'm sorry."

"Yeah, I know *exactly* how it is." Naveah headed toward the track gate.

"Wait! I'll tell 'em all the truth right now," Kareem offered, grabbing his phone.

"No!" Naveah insisted. "I'm over it and done with those girls. I'm focused on cross country right now, and I don't need you or anyone talking about me again. Just drop it, okay?"

Naveah ducked under the chain and ran off, never looking back.

The summer rushed by. Naveah ran almost every day—sometimes at Baldwin Hill and sometimes in a loop she and Mom created that circled behind Bluford High to nearby East Park and then back home. Despite the heat and a few days in which distant wildfires filled the air with a hazy smoke, Naveah grew stronger as the weeks passed.

Mom had been training, too, Naveah noticed. She now skillfully used the walker to move herself from room to room without too much trouble. She also drank protein drinks regularly and took her medicines without protest, and she even chatted with Naveah about running tips and strategies. But instead of getting better, she seemed to be slowly weakening. The time each day in which she was out of bed and had energy to talk was diminishing, and her appetite had not returned.

Dad made sure that Christian spent his days in summer camp at Little Learning Spot, and the hospital had arranged for a private duty nurse, Mattie Wills, to check on Mom twice a week. Time passed and the visits helped, but nothing increased Mom's energy.

Noticing how exhausted Mom was, Dad pulled the wheelchair from the closet and parked it in the living room where she could reach it.

"Amaya, maybe we should…" he began softly, but Mom shook her head.

"No. I'm taking Naveah to tryouts, and I don't need no wheelchair to do it," Mom insisted. "Bad enough that I have to use this thing," she said, glaring at the walker.

Dad eyed Naveah, but no one said anything until Christian spoke up.

"It's okay, Mom," he said encouragingly. "I can help you. I'll push you wherever you want to go."

"Thank you, baby," Mom said, giving him a hug, her eyes glistening slightly. "But I'm not there yet."

A few days before tryouts, Mom told Nurse Wills that her back was sore. The nurse gave her an extra painkiller that seemed to relieve the pain, but Mom slipped into an unusually deep sleep on the living room sofa at dinner time.

Watching her chest rise and fall, Naveah was struck by how small she had become. Once broad-shouldered and strong, she had withered over the summer.

"I don't know about tryouts, Naveah," Dad said, seeming to read her thoughts. Where Mom lost weight, he had gained it. His face was now gray and doughy, and his uniform shirts often looked tight and uncomfortable, as if he were storing stress and worry inside them.

"Your running has been great for her, and I know she really wants to be there for you, but she's really struggling now," he explained. "We'll get results from Mom's tests soon to see if these treatments are helping but . . . I can't see how she can leave the house like this, baby."

Naveah couldn't argue. She always knew of the possibility that Mom would be unable to join her on Baldwin Hill, but she had held out hope that Mom would rally. That the medicine would work, and her appetite would return. That they would get ice cream at Scoops again like they used to in summertime. But none of it happened.

"Feel better, Mom," Naveah whispered as Dad finished the dinner dishes before picking up another night shift.

Mom snored lightly but otherwise didn't seem to move or budge. Naveah shuddered at her stillness. Even Christian seemed to notice. He sat on the floor playing Minecraft with his earbuds in but stopped several times to look at her.

"Is Mom gonna be okay?" he asked finally. His eyes glistened in the blue glare of the TV screen.

"Yeah, she's just sleeping," Naveah said, joining him on the floor.

"That's all she does anymore," he said, fidgeting with the controller. "I miss her."

"Me too," she replied. Naveah recognized Chriveah, their old world in Minecraft, on the TV screen. The land had been changed dramatically since the last time she had seen it.

The rolling green orchards that they once crafted together were gone. Roads that used to connect their two kingdoms had vanished, buried under high stone walls that towered over the countryside. Behind the walls in a lonely corner stood Christian's small house, the same one he had built when they used to play together, only now it was encircled by a ring of fire.

"What happened to our world, Chris?" Naveah asked, feeling a pang of guilt. She knew it took him many hours to make these changes, perhaps longer. Yet she had not even noticed him doing it. She realized she could not remember the last time she sat with him and gave him undivided attention. "Why all these walls and fires?"

"That's to keep out the sickness," he explained, his words making her wince. "And the creepers and stuff too."

Watching him, Naveah could see that Mom's illness had been stressing him too, though he had hidden it. She cursed herself for not noticing sooner. Then she grabbed the other remote and sat down next to him.

Christian had left a tiny part of her side of Chriveah unchanged. Starting at her cottage, she added a walking path that matched the color of Bluford's track. She snaked it through a nearby forest, around a pond, and up to the base of a mountain just like her running path at Baldwin Hill. She then carved a tunnel through the mountains. She continued the path on the other side, installing hidden steps that climbed his walls so the path led directly from her cottage to his.

"What's that?" he asked, studying it carefully.

"It's a secret running path that connects me and you," she said proudly, rubbing the back of his head. "This way we can always find each other, no matter what. Got it?"

Christian didn't say anything, but Naveah noticed that for the rest of the night he didn't destroy her pathway. And later, his eyes growing heavy, he added torches along the path she had created.

"That's so we can see in the dark," he explained, giving her a little hug as he went to bed.

The night before tryouts, Naveah couldn't sleep. Anxious and fidgety, she organized her room and watched animal videos on YouTube until even they began to bore her, yet she still could not relax. Finally, in the lonely dark well past midnight, she reinstalled the apps she had deleted weeks ago.

Notifications from Snapchat, Instagram, and TikTok flashed on her phone along with a flood of direct messages that she had never read. The latest one was from Kareem from two days ago.

Hope you're good. Just wanted you to know Jonique is going out for cross country! You get a rematch. You got this!!! ⚡⚡⚡

An electric jolt of adrenaline surged through Naveah's body.

"What!" she exclaimed, sitting up in her bed.

Tryouts at Baldwin Hill already loomed over her. But with Jonique going out for the team, the stakes were higher. The hype in school, the trash talking, the comments on social media, and all the drama. She knew it would spark like wildfire at tryouts. There was no way to stop it.

Naveah reread Kareem's message and noticed there were others he had sent that she had never seen.

Where you at? said one on the morning of the race. **You okay?**

Later he had sent an apology for doubting her. Then one of his friends at school, Lionel Shephard, sent a screenshot that showed Kareem defending her in a chat where someone had called her a liar and a coward.

He got your back, Lionel had written. The images showed Kareem sticking up for her.

Nah, she ain't like that. Don't hate. He said this more than once. She noticed a few of his posts were followed by mean comments from some of Jonique's friends.

Naveah thanked Lionel and realized she had been wrong to shut out Kareem all summer. She noticed a final unread message from him last week included a photo on Instagram from Bluford's football team.

It featured several older students she recognized from school—Cooper Hodden, Roylin Bailey, Hakeem Randall. But on the near side in the second row stood Kareem smiling proudly.

Congratulations to our new varsity team! the post read. He had made it! Pride surged through her heart. She knew he had worked hard all summer, maybe harder than any student she knew.

See what Baldwin Hill did for me. You too? You got this! ⚡⚡⚡, he commented in the note to her.

She left a ♡ on his football post and then answered all his DMs.

Congratulations on varsity! 🎉 👏

Then she added:

Sorry—been offline for a while.

And a second later:

Thanks for having my back. Wish me luck tomorrow—or later today. 😬

She hit send and stared at the phone, hoping for an answer, but it was after 2:00 a.m. and for once Kareem was not there.

BEEP. BEEP. BEEP.

The blaring of Naveah's alarm jerked her awake from a black, dreamless sleep. She glanced at the screen. It was 6:45 a.m. She had slept for only a few hours, and it felt like even less. Still, she wanted to get to Baldwin Hill early to warm up, just like Mom had coached her.

And now Jonique would be there! She still couldn't believe it.

Naveah hurried to the bathroom to wash and then slipped on her shorts and T-shirt, taking extra care to lace and tie her sneakers.

Would Mom be coming? Naveah hoped so, especially now that the race had become personal. She crept to the door and knocked lightly.

"Mom?" she called, but no reply came. "You up?"

Naveah opened the door slightly. She hoped to find her mother sitting on the side of the bed, trying to muster the strength to reach for the walker. But instead, she was sound asleep.

"Mom?"

A tiny flinch shook the blankets as Naveah approached the bed. Fluffy wisps of hair peeked out from under Mom's scarf, yet she seemed smaller than ever, as if she had shrunk overnight.

Naveah gazed down at her sleeping mother. Without an alarm to wake her, she seemed to have forgotten completely about the tryouts. Even if she had gotten up, what could she do in her condition? Everything Naveah had read about pancreatic cancer seemed to be unfolding no matter how hard Mom fought.

It's not fair. Naveah's thoughts stormed in her head as she sat on the edge of the mattress in the heavy morning quiet.

For a moment, Mom half opened her eyes and gazed at Naveah as if she didn't know who she was.

"Oh," she breathed. "Oh…hey, baby…I'm so tired…what time is it?"

Tears tried to gather in Naveah's eyes, but she willed them back. Mom shouldn't go anywhere. Naveah's could see that. "It's really early, Mama. You rest," she said.

Mom nodded and closed her eyes.

Part of Naveah wanted to skip the tryouts, lie down next to her and cry. But a bigger part felt ready to run harder than she ever had. She would run for both of them.

"I'ma do this, Mama," she whispered. "Jonique's gonna be there too."

Mom's brows stirred slightly as Naveah kissed her cheek, soft as old paper, and walked out.

Chapter 9

"I'm sorry, Naveah," her father said when she dashed into the kitchen. He was slouched forward at his chair smelling of sweat and cardboard. She knew he had just returned from his night shift and would be going to bed shortly. "You know she wanted to be there today."

"I know," Naveah replied, trying to force the sadness from her mind.

Focus, she told herself. She grabbed a banana and quickly gulped down some orange juice.

"She'd been thinking about it for weeks, but she just doesn't have it in her right now," he added.

"I know, Dad. I saw her." Naveah grabbed her phone and headed toward the door.

Focus, she told herself again. But the sad image of Mom crumpled in bed kept clouding her thoughts as her father continued, talking as much to himself as to her.

"We always knew these treatments would be rough. If they worked, they would buy her some time. That's what she wanted. But if we knew it would be like this," Dad shrugged. He fished his phone from his pocket and placed it on the cluttered table. "Docs are supposed to call this morning to discuss her latest tests. We'll see…"

In that moment, Naveah spotted something in her father she had never noticed. For the first time, he seemed fragile too.

The sight burned in her mind as he swallowed hard and seemed to regain himself.

"Whatever it is, we'll take it one day at a time, right baby? What else can we do?"

His words made sense, but Naveah couldn't listen. The somber kitchen. Dad's tired voice. Mom's labored sleeping. It was all too much.

Naveah had to get out. She had to move. To push back, whether it be against cancer or Jonique or anything that added more pain to a world already full of hurt.

"I gotta go," she huffed, dashing out the door.

"Good luck today," Dad called out. "I know you'll do great."

Naveah rushed to the bus stop, her stomach a tangle of nerves.

Overhead, the morning sun blazed, promising to scald the entire city in a few hours. The ten-minute wait for the crowded bus seemed like an eternity, but the rattling stop-and-go ride through morning traffic to Baldwin Hill felt even longer. When the bus finally hissed to a stop at the base of the hill, Naveah knew she did not have time to do her full warmup. Again, nerves scrambled her stomach and made her legs tremble with energy.

A handful of runners had already gathered at the starting point of the running trail when Naveah finally joined them.

"Naveah? Is that you?" a familiar voice asked.

Naveah turned around to see Ms. Sherman weaving through the runners toward her. She wore shorts, a Bluford Cross Country T-shirt, and yellow running shoes instead of her usual teacher clothes. A silver coach's whistle dangled from her neck, and she clutched a clipboard under her arm. In the bright sunshine, the smiling teacher almost seemed like a different person from the one who had taken away her phone at the end of the school year.

"Hey, Ms. Sherman," Naveah said.

"I'm so glad you're here," the teacher beamed. "How's your summer going?"

"It's been...okay," Naveah stammered, not wanting to explain, especially now.

Ms. Sherman squinted for a second as if she saw something that concerned her, but then someone interrupted, and she stepped away to greet other runners.

"I'm happy you decided to join us too, Jonique," the coach said. "We might have a champion team this year in cross *and* track."

Jonique gave the coach a weak smile until she passed, but then rolled her eyes dramatically at Naveah as if she were trash.

"Girl, why are you even here?" Jonique scoffed. "You know you can't beat me. That's why you didn't show up that day. Shoulda stayed home today, too. Whole school's gonna watch this one. Sasha's makin' sure of that." She pointed to a girl standing at the edge of the crowd aiming a phone at them. "Maybe you should use your mama as an excuse again and go home."

Naveah's blood boiled. "What's your problem?" she fumed. "I got as much right to be here as you, and if I win—"

"You ain't gonna win. Our team is solid without you, and I'm working on a D1 scholarship. I am not about to let you mess all that up. So tell everyone your mama is sick or whatever you need to do, and leave."

"But it's—"

The piercing blast of the coach's whistle sliced through the air. Instantly, the group of runners, now two dozen strong, moved to the foot of Baldwin Hill where Coach Sherman stood, whistle in hand, waving them forward.

Jonique rushed off to join them, and Naveah followed close behind.

"Welcome to cross country tryouts!" the coach boomed. "It's great to see so many familiar faces... and so many new ones too. That's how teams are built, and that's what we want here—Bluford's *team*." Naveah tried to listen as the coach went over the tryout details. She learned they would be running in groups of three, and that the course began and ended at the bottom of Baldwin Hill, a loop of 5K. Naveah nodded and shook out her legs, eyeing Jonique the whole time.

"If all goes well, this should be your slowest run all season. Why? Because we will train you and make you faster each week in practice," the coach explained. "Today's goal is to get a baseline of your speed, your commitment, and what you bring to the table." The coach then droned on about JV and varsity details, but Naveah had stopped listening.

All the chatter didn't matter, not today, not for this race. No matter what anyone said, Naveah knew it was time to settle the score with Jonique once and for all—for everyone to see, even if Mom couldn't be there. Even if she never got to see her run in person.

"So take a few minutes to stretch and warm up," the coach concluded. "Then divide up into threes, and give us your best run, ladies. We'll record your times at the end!"

A small crowd of parents, friends, and spectators had gathered in the lot at the base of the hill by the starting line. They would have a perfect view of the runners as they sprinted to the finish. Naveah figured she knew some of the onlookers from school but she blotted them out. Her thoughts were on someone else. Scanning the group of runners, she found Jonique at the edge of the crowd stretching. Her friend Sasha filmed her.

"It's about to go down," Jonique was saying when Naveah stepped in front of the camera.

"I'ma run in your heat today," Naveah stated calmly. "I hope everyone's watching."

Jonique's jaw dropped. Sasha stopped filming, but Naveah didn't care.

"They might not like you, but they will respect you," Mom had said. Naveah would prove it.

"All right. On my mark," Coach Sherman called out then, holding up her whistle and locking eyes with the first three runners.

With a quick screeching blast, the first heat took off. Naveah's limbs tingled as she hovered by the starting area watching each group of runners launch up the hill. Finally, Jonique approached with Teresa Ortiz, a mid-distance runner from the track team.

"Next group, get set," Coach Sherman barked. Naveah moved into position between Teresa and Jonique. For a second the coach eyed them.

"Remember, ladies. Pace yourselves. This is a baseline run, not a race," she said with a sly smile, as if she already knew they weren't going to listen.

Despite the building heat, Naveah's hands were cold and clammy. Charged with adrenaline, her pulse began to pump like a piston in her neck. The quiet before the start seemed to stretch out and slow down until . . .

WHIRRRR! Coach Sherman's whistle screamed into the air.

Teresa bolted forward, taking the lead immediately and setting a blistering pace. Jonique slipped right behind her, throwing an elbow that caught Naveah in the chest and made her shift back a step. Almost instantly, the trail began to pitch upward. Heat from the rocky pathway blasted the runners as they climbed.

Teresa was quick, much faster than Naveah expected, but she knew the pace was impossible to maintain. Several runs up and down Baldwin Hill had taught her that. Jonique seemed to know it too. She tucked in behind Teresa and let her lead, not once trying to pass her or even match her stride as they ascended the steaming hill.

Bits of gravel and stone scattered as the trail zigzagged higher. Careful to control her breathing, Naveah felt her heart rate beginning to spike and her legs starting to ache as they reached a sharp bend. Naveah knew Jonique's strategy and what was coming. Jonique was running smart, hanging back, storing her energy, and waiting for the right time to break out into a sprint. To win, Naveah knew she would have to do it too. Yet already, just keeping up with them, she was starting to feel fatigue. Her lungs wanted more oxygen. Her lips wanted water. Her legs wanted a break.

No, she told them all. *Not now.*

Just then Teresa's foot clipped a rock, causing her to stumble awkwardly. Jonique just managed to avoid her as she tripped sideways into Naveah. The collision was minor, but it broke Naveah's stride and stole her momentum.

"Sorry," Teresa huffed, as she gasped for air and grabbed at her ankle.

Naveah stepped past her to see Jonique accelerating. The disruption had given her a solid lead, and now she was pulling the trigger, exploding up the hill like a rocket as clouds of dust erupted at her feet. Naveah watched her disappear around a switchback and knew she was in trouble.

No!

Desperation stung Naveah's eyes. Her hopes of beating Jonique were fading. Maybe Jonique was right. Maybe Naveah could never beat her. Maybe she just wasn't good enough for the cross country team. Maybe this tryout had been a mistake, a fantasy she and Mom created to cope with cancer. Naveah knew she could end it by just stopping. That would cease the burning pain in her legs and chest. She could just walk the rest of the way and be done with it. She imagined telling Mom the news.

Mom of a year ago might have shown her disappointment. But today? As frail and tired as she seemed, Mom would barely notice. She would just go back to sleep and say, "It don't matter."

But Naveah knew it did. She remembered how happy it made Mom to know she was trying out for the team. The glint in her eyes had been real, a small joy they discovered at a time they needed it, when so much else had gone wrong. To give up now, Naveah knew, would make it all meaningless. It would be accepting failure when Mom had taught her to fight. Not only would Naveah be letting Mom down, she would be letting herself down too.

Naveah's legs burned. Her chest throbbed. Her lungs were starved for oxygen. And now, deep in her heart, she felt a river of sorrow for her mother. There was so little she could control, so few things she could do for her mom. But running. She could still do that, at least for a little while longer.

The path ahead shifted and dipped. Naveah knew it was the spot where she had run into Kareem so long ago. That meant she was almost at the top. The rest of the run would be downhill. Easier, if she could reach it.

Not gonna quit, Mama, not gonna quit. She repeated the words like a prayer in her mind. Maybe there was no hope of catching Jonique or making the team. But she could still finish strong, still fight to the last step.

The trail began to flatten beneath her feet. Suddenly the sky expanded, and she was on top of Baldwin Hill. A slight breeze kissed her face as she passed where she and Kareem once stood together alone above the city.

Let's finish this, she told herself, pushing ahead.

Immediately, the ground began to tilt downward. Suddenly gravity, which fought her the whole way up, now drew her forward and urged her to go faster. Naveah answered, picking up her pace and allowing her momentum to build. Pushed by the downward slope, her feet churned over the dusty path, and Naveah accelerated. With the breeze in her face and the trail winding out before her, Naveah suddenly felt airborne, like she was some winged creature flying down the hill.

The parking area and visitor center appeared in the distance. All that was left was the final straightaway, just a quarter mile or so and she would reach the finish line. Suddenly Jonique came into view. She was only about twenty yards ahead. *Not close*, Naveah thought. *Not yet.*

Naveah stretched her legs and threw herself into an all-out sprint. Jonique's back inched closer. Naveah's pain was real now and impossible to ignore. Fire burned her muscles, and her vision dimmed with effort. But she knew the end was coming. It was right there.

And she was still flying.

With a glance at the parking lot, she saw a familiar Honda with a young boy standing next to it jumping and screaming at the top of his lungs. In front of him was a wheelchair with a tiny woman hunched inside holding her slender fist in the air. A man stood nearby clapping and hooting.

It was her family, Naveah realized. They had come for her. They'd made it. Mom had kept her promise. She had fought through her suffering to be there for her.

Her eyes stinging from sweat and tears, Naveah dug deeper, pushed harder, and began to close the distance with Jonique. In the electric blur of Christian's screams, Dad's cheers, Mom's fist, and another familiar figure, Kareem, urging her forward, Naveah matched Jonique's stride. She propelled herself right up to the champion runner, shoulder to shoulder, almost step for step as they reached and finally crossed the finish line.

"Jonique at 21:49, Naveah at 21:50. The best times of tryouts so far, girls," the coach hollered as they passed. Jonique raised an arm in victory and collapsed on a nearby bench, but Naveah trotted ahead, bleary-eyed and wobbly, into the parking lot to the people who had come to cheer for her.

"You came, Mom! You guys came," she said, hugging her mother's slight frame.

"Of course I did, baby," Mom whispered. "I heard you mention Jonique this morning. I had to show up. Your brother...he helped me with the chair."

"I'm sorry I didn't win," Naveah said to them all. Tears of sorrow and gratitude and love rolled down her cheeks. Mom had them too.

"Are you kidding? Look around. You won, baby. I'm so proud of you," Mom whispered. "You're my champion."

"You're mine too, Mom. Always."

They hugged for several long moments at Baldwin Hill, the frail woman in her wheelchair, and her family.

People who had filmed the race turned off their cameras and hushed their voices. Kareem flashed a heart sign to Naveah from a distance before leaving them. Other athletes and even Coach Sherman, who had come to congratulate her, decided not to intrude and left the family alone.

Even Jonique shed a tear in the parking lot and posted one word on her social media channels and on Naveah's page, something that spread at Bluford High faster than any gossip, quicker than lightning:

Respect. ⚡⚡⚡♡♡♡

Epilogue

That night, with Mom resting in her chair and the family gathered around, Dad made an announcement. Christian paused his video game, and Naveah put down her phone after texting Kareem about meeting up for ice cream at Scoops.

"I spoke with Dr. Lim this morning," he said, his voice wavering with emotion. "Mom's aggressive treatments have stopped her cancer from spreading. She's not out of the woods. But this buys her some time. They're gonna pause her treatments for a few weeks and let her recover her strength. So, for now, we got good news. She's still fighting," he said, wiping his eyes. "She's still fighting. We still got her."

Days later, when it became official that she had made the cross country team, Naveah shared the news with Mom and decided to make a final post so everyone knew the truth.

Kareem recorded while she spoke without filters or masks or effects: "My mom has pancreatic cancer. She's had it all summer, and we don't know how much longer we'll have her."

Naveah swallowed hard and forced herself to continue:

> In these posts, we get so mean to each other sometimes. We tell lies, too. I've seen it. Maybe I've done it. Whatever, I just don't want to be part of it anymore.
>
> Life is too short. My mom is teaching me that. At the end of the day, no one will look back on their life and wish they posted more or spent more time on their phones. Instead they gonna wish they *did* more. Saw more. Got out more, you know. Lived their lives. That's what I'm gonna do.
>
> Running makes me happy. It makes my mom happy too. That's what I'm gonna do for now. So if you're looking for Lightning Legs, don't look here no more. Look for me on the track or on the trail. I'll be on the run. See you out there.

Naveah's hands shook as she posted the video. They trembled, too, as she went on to delete each social media app on her phone.

"You sure you want to do that?" Kareem asked as he watched her.

Naveah nodded. She had never felt more certain. "Definitely," she answered, shutting down her phone and raising her eyes from the small screen to meet Kareem's gaze. He smiled back.

"You wanna go get that ice cream now?"

"I'll race you there," she grinned, rushing past him.

"Hold up! That's cheating!" he shouted, chasing after her.

Together they dashed down the street, laughing under the warm afternoon sun.

Neither of them noticed Naveah's post going viral.

The popular Bluford classic has been supercharged in a NEW illustrated edition!

Featuring 28 original sketches from
Gerald Purnell, cover artist for the Bluford Series,
The Bully: Illustrated Edition will hook
readers from the very first page—
and leave them on the edge of their
seats to the very last.